Lone Star Ranger:

Volume 3

A Ranger to Fight With

James J. Griffin

Lone Star Ranger: Vol.3
A Ranger to Fight With by James J. Griffin
Copyright© 2014 James J. Griffin
Texas Ranger badge image courtesy of the Texas Ranger
Hall of Fame and Museum, Waco
Author photo credited to Susanne Onatah

Yankee Cowboy Press
Keene, NH 03431
www.yankeecowboypress.com
yankeecowboypress@yahoo.com
All rights reserved.
ISBN: 9798342228312

DEDICATION
For my cousins,
Jane Tompkins and Larry Griffin

Prologue

Nate Stewart lay on his bunk, staring at the ceiling of his tent. His three Texas Ranger tentmates, Hoot Harrison, who had quickly befriended Nate, Jim Kelly, and Dan Morton, were all sleeping, snoring softly. However, Nate was having trouble falling asleep.

Tomorrow, the Rangers would break camp and head for the Big Bend. That meant Nate would be riding with them, leaving behind the ranch where his father, mother, and older brother had been murdered by outlaws, and Nate himself left for dead. The men responsible were still out there somewhere, and Nate was determined to see them brought to justice. However, that would have to wait.

The Ranger company he was with had been ordered to far West Texas, and he had no choice but to go with them. Already, everything which could be packed ahead of time was bundled up, most of the supplies loaded in George Bayfield's chuck wagon.

At first light, the men would eat a quick breakfast, the tents would be taken down, and everything loaded on pack mules. An hour after sunrise, they would be on the trail, heading west.

Nate sighed as he thought back on everything that had

happened to him in the past few weeks; how unexpectedly his life had changed. He had moved with his family from a home in Wilmington, Delaware to a small ranch outside San Saba, Texas.

After the attack which left Nate an orphan, he had been found and nursed back to health by a company of Texas Rangers. With no family or friends in Texas, it appeared Nate would have to move back to Delaware, to live with his aunt, uncle, and eight cousins. However, fate had taken a hand when Jeb Rollins, the Ranger arranging for his trip home, had been confronted by a group of rustlers.

In the ensuing gunfight, Nate had saved Jeb's life by tackling and knocking out one of the gunmen, before he could shoot the Ranger. Jeb decided Nate had enough guts, and potential, to be taken on as a camp helper for his Ranger company, despite Nate's age of only fourteen.

I've learned how to use a gun since then, Nate thought, *to care for and ride a horse, and how to handle myself with my fists... not to mention takin' on someone in a knife fight. I'll sure never forget what Hoot taught me about that.*

I've shot a couple of men, and been shot and nearly killed myself. If I hadn't stuffed my train tickets and the rest of my papers back in my shirt pocket, then forgotten about them, the bullet which hit me in the chest would've killed me. Even at that, I'm real lucky those papers managed to stop that slug.

I've tried smokin', which I doubt I'll try again, drunk tequila and whiskey, learned how to play cards, and thought about huggin' and kissin' a girl.

He softly chuckled. *He—I mean, heck, I've even learned how to cuss some. My ma'd sure have washed out my mouth with soap if she ever heard me doin' that.*

I helped stop a bank robbery, and made some good friends. I only wish I'd caught up with the men who killed my folks.

I've had two more run-ins with 'em since, even managed to put a bullet into that pale-eyed son of Satan who leads the gang, but they're still on the loose, after killin' some of my partners, and more innocent folks.

Nate sighed again. *After all that, I'm still not certain what I'll do when I have to come face to face with a man, over leveled six-guns. I don't know if I'll be able to pull the trigger under those circumstances.*

And for my pards to count on me, I need to be a Ranger they can fight with.

With those thoughts, he drifted into an uneasy sleep.

1

Nate was amazed at how quickly camp was broken once breakfast had been eaten. He was assigned to help George wash up the dishes and pans, then pack those and the rest of the cooking utensils and foodstuffs in the chuck wagon.

While he and George did that, the other Rangers took down the tents and cots, then rolled up the tents and folded the cots, and got everything loaded on the pack mules.

Nate watched while George hitched two mules to the wagon, and listened to him explain how it was done. He gave the cook a hand getting some of the harness and lines in place.

"I don't expect you to be able to hitch a team the first time you try it, Nate," George said. "In fact, most of these boys don't have a clue how to hitch and drive a team. However, it'd be a good thing for you to know, if you're willin' to learn how."

"I sure am," Nate answered. "I figure everything I can learn will help me be a good Ranger, once I'm old enough to be taken on as a regular member."

At fourteen, Nate was four years too young to actually

join the Texas Rangers. However, seeing the boy's willing-ness to learn, his natural intelligence, and his courage, Captain Dave Quincy had deliberately marked Nate's en-listment papers "Birth Date Unknown", and put him on as a probationary Ranger, instead of just a camp helper.

It wasn't the first time the Rangers had bent the rules, nor would it be the last. In fact, while everyone believed Hoot Harrison had fibbed about his age when he signed on with the Rangers two years ago, claiming to be eighteen when he was only sixteen, they didn't know how young he actually was.

The truth was, Hoot had also been Nate's age, only fourteen, when he enlisted. Hoot had confided the fact he was just now sixteen to Nate, and no one else.

"That's the attitude to take," George said. "Listen, we're just about finished here. You'd better go saddle your horse. One thing Cap'n Dave really don't like is a man who's not prepared on time, and holds up the rest of the outfit. You'll be in for a real butt-chewin' if you ain't in the saddle when the other men are ready to ride out."

"All right, George, and thanks. Reckon I'll get Big Red."

Nate hurried over to the rope corral. Shorty Beach was just beginning to take it down, as most of the other men had already roped out their mounts, and were saddling them.

"Mornin', son," he said. "Been wonderin' where the heck you were at. Can't take these ropes down until eve-ryone has his horse."

"Good mornin', Shorty. George kept me a little longer than I thought he would," Nate answered.

"That'd be George all right," Shorty said, with a laugh. "Well, you'd better get a move on. Most of the other boys are already saddled up."

"Okay." Nate got Red's lead rope, ducked into the

corral, and whistled. He'd been working on getting Red to answer his call for the past several weeks. Red picked up his head, nickered, and trotted up to Nate. He nuzzled the boy's chest.

"Good boy, Red," Nate praised him. He took a piece of left-over biscuit from his shirt pocket and gave it to the sorrel. Red took the treat, then nuzzled Nate's hand for more.

"Oh, no, ya don't," Nate said, chuckling. "That's enough for now. C'mon, we've gotta get ready to ride."

Nate led Red out of the corral, over to where the saddles, bridles, and gear were kept. He took the currycomb and brush from his saddlebags, along with the hoof pick.

He gave Red a quick brushing, checked his hooves to make sure they were cleaned out, with no pebbles which could possibly cripple the horse stuck between the sole and frog, then replaced everything in his saddlebags. He threw the blanket and saddle on Red's back, making doubly certain his cinches were tight, then slipped the headstall over Red's ears and the bit in his mouth.

He picked up the reins and swung into the saddle, then headed over to where the other Rangers, except Shorty and George, were assembling into a side-by-side column. With the addition of Carl Swan, Lee Shelton, and Larry Cannon to their ranks, Captain Quincy's company now numbered eighteen men, still two short of its usual complement of twenty.

"There you be, Nate," Hoot Harrison called. "Fall in alongside me."

Hoot was at the rear of the line, mounted on his lineback dun, Dusty. Nate reined in alongside him. Big Red, not accustomed to being part of such a large number of horses, snorted his excitement. He tossed his head, stamped his feet, and reared slightly. With a quick tug on the reins, Nate pulled him back down.

"Settle down, Red," he ordered, then spun the gelding in a circle, three times. Red snorted, but stood quietly in place.

"I see you're learnin' how to handle a horse real good, Nate," Jeb Rollins praised.

"You and Red are good teachers," Nate answered.

Shorty Beach finished taking down the rope corral and loading its pieces on one of the pack mules. He joined the rest of the men, while George rolled his wagon up alongside them.

"We're all present and accounted for, Cap'n," Shorty said.

"I can see that," Quincy answered. "And may I speak for the entire company when I say we greatly appreciate the fact you're finally wearing new drawers under your denims. Perhaps now any renegades we're hunting won't smell you comin' from a mile away."

"Don't thank me," Shorty retorted. "Thank those two young whippersnappers hidin' at the back of the line. If they hadn't tossed my old ones in the river I'd still be wearin' 'em. These new woolies are makin' my butt itch. They scratch like the devil."

"Better your butt itches than my nose closes up and my eyes water from the stink of your old drawers," Dakota Stevens said, to general laughter from the rest of the men.

"All right, that's enough. It's time to settle down and get ready to head out," Quincy said. "Most of you already know this, but it bears repeatin', especially for the new men. We'll be pushin' as hard and fast as we can until we reach the Big Bend territory. That means ridin' from sunup to sundown, with only a quick break for dinner and a couple of short stops to allow the horses a breather. Except for today.

"It's only about twenty miles from here to Menardville. We'll ride that far today, and camp outside town tonight. We should reach there a couple of hours before sundown. Everyone will have the chance to spend some time in town. That'll give those of you who need to pick up any personal supplies the opportunity to do so.

"It'll also be your last easy day's ride until we get where we're headed. After tonight, we won't see another town until we reach Fort Stockton. That's another two hundred or so miles west of Menardville.

"I intend to cover those two hundred miles in a week, or less. And after that, depending on exactly where we head into the Big Bend, it'll be another hundred to hundred and fifty miles of real hard ridin'.

"Any of you new men who think you can't keep up, say so right now. I'll give you a discharge, no questions asked and no hard feelings."

There was a general shaking of heads and muttered "nos" from Nate, Carl, Larry, and Lee.

"Fine. I knew I could count on all of you. One last thing before we move out. Nate, Phil, come on up here."

Nate looked at Hoot, puzzled.

"Wonder what the cap'n wants with me?" he whispered.

"There's only one way to find out. Go on up there," Hoot answered.

"I guess you're right." Nate lifted his reins and heeled Big Red into a walk. He rode to the front of the column and stopped next to Captain Quincy. Phil Knight was already alongside the captain.

"You wanted to see me, Cap'n?" Nate said.

"I certainly did," Quincy replied. "You're gonna be partnered with Phil today, and probably for the next few. He's our head wrangler, who's in charge of the *remuda*."

"The *remuda*? What's that?" Nate asked.

"It's Spanish. A *remuda* is the extra horses and mules," Phil explained. "On a ranch, every cowboy has a string of horses, owned by the ranch, assigned to him. Very few cowboys actually own a personal mount. All those horses, taken together, are the *remuda*, especially when the crew is on a cattle drive.

"Every big ranch, and even quite a few of the fair to middlin' sized ones, has at least one horse wrangler, mebbe more, dependin' on the size of the spread. They're in charge of the horses, breakin' new ones to ride, figurin' out what a horse will do best, like bein' a ropin' or cuttin' horse, for example."

"A ropin' or cuttin' horse?"

"Yup. A ropin' horse does just what the term says. It's real good at chasin' down cows for its rider to rope. A cuttin' horse is an expert at separatin' one cow from the rest of the herd, say for doctorin' or brandin', and keepin' it from headin' back to the rest of the cattle.

"Most cuttin' horses, once you let 'em loose on a cow critter, will turn on a nickel and give you change, and you can bet the man ridin' 'em better be ready for every twist and turn they make, or he'll find himself eatin' dirt. A man ridin' a good cuttin' horse mostly just hangs on and goes along for the ride.

"Anyway, to get back on track, on a cattle drive, or when us Rangers, or any outfit, are headin' somewhere, the wrangler's in charge of the *remuda*. He has to make sure none of the horses stray, and that they keep up with the rest of the outfit. And when we bed down for the night, the wrangler's in charge of all the horses, not just the spare ones."

"So, the cowboy takin' care of the horses is called a wrangler," Nate said.

"Hold on right there, son," Phil answered. "A cowboy is

a cowboy, and a wrangler is a wrangler. It's a downright insult to call a wrangler a cowboy, and vice versa. Them's fightin' words, even if they do oftentimes help each other out.

"You might see a wrangler work with cattle for a bit, and a cowboy with horses, but they ain't hardly the same thing a'tall. I'm not talkin' about just ridin' a horse, naturally. Every cowboy rides. I'm talkin' about breakin' a horse to saddle, and trainin' it to be a good cow pony or ridin' horse. That's the wrangler's job."

"I'm sorry, Phil," Nate said. "I didn't realize there was a difference."

"There's no need to apologize, Nate. Most Easterners don't know the difference, until they've been out here a spell," Quincy said. "Heck, I'm positive there's even plenty of city folks right here in Texas who don't have a clue about the difference between a horse wrangler and a cowboy. But that's enough palaverin'.

"Phil, you can explain more to Nate while he's ridin' with you. Nate, the reason I'm having you ride with Phil is because you seem to have a real way with horses, at least with yours. I'm wagering you'll make a fine wrangler. Phil's a real top hand with horses, so pay close attention to what he tells you. You can learn a lot from him. You have any questions?"

"Not right now, Cap'n. But I'm certain I will," Nate answered.

"Good. Phil?"

"None at all, Cap'n."

"Fine. You two head back to where we've got the *remuda*, in that small box *arroyo*, and gather 'em. The rest of you, ride on out. Rangers, company ho!"

With a wave of his hand, Quincy started the column in motion.

"Follow me, Nate," Phil ordered. He put Parker, his rangy chestnut, into a trot. Nate matched Red's pace to Parker's. A few minutes later, they were at the mouth of a small *arroyo*, where the *remuda* was being held. A rope tied to a redberry juniper at each side of the *arroyo* and stretched across its mouth prevented the horses and mules from straying.

"Nate," Phil said. "Bein' in charge of the *remuda's* usually not all that hard. Horses and mules are herd animals, so they'll mostly stick with their buddies, not only for protection from mountain lions or wolves and such, but also for each other's company. These animals we have here are used to travelin' with us, so they'll follow along docilely enough, for the most part. Once in a while one of 'em'll decide to quit the bunch and wander off on his own, or stop to nibble, instead of keepin' up. It's our job to chase any bunch-quitters or stragglers back with the rest."

"Kinda like when Watson got spooked by the longhorn at the Lopez spread, and I had to catch him?" Nate asked.

"Yeah, like that. From what I hear tell, you did a fine job roundin' up that mule. Hoot was right pleased you did. However, it'll be a lot easier to stop a runaway once you learn how to rope. I'll be showin' you the basics of that over the next few days. But becomin' a top hand with a rope is just like bein' an expert with a six-gun. It takes lots of practice, so you'll need to work on your ropin' every chance you get."

"I'll do just that," Nate promised.

"Good. Now, there's just one more thing before we start the *remuda* movin'. Don't ever underestimate a horse or mule, even a donkey or burro. Most folks think horses are dumb, and mules just stubborn, with no brains a'tall. Lemme tell you, when you love horses as much as I do, and have worked with 'em as long as I have, you'll find out

14

just how clever they are.

"Horses are downright smart, and what people think is stubbornness on a mule's part is just his way of sayin' what you're askin' him to do makes no sense, at least by his lights, or is mebbe even downright dangerous. Out here, a man needs to rely on his horse for his very life. Learn to read your horse. Watch Red's ears, feel his muscles under you. Watch how he holds his head, even his tail.

"As we ride along, I'll tell you what to look for, and explain what the signs your horse is givin' you mean. If you don't learn anythin' else from me, learn this much. Trust your horse's instincts, fully and completely. If he balks, there's almost always a good reason for it. What looks like solid ground to you might very well be a patch of quicksand, ready to swallow up both your horse and you. Your horse can sense that. He ain't gonna get stuck in mud, get swept away in a river and drowned, or fall down a steep slope and break his neck, less'n he's forced to by a rider who don't know better, or thinks he's smarter than his horse."

He leaned forward in the saddle and patted his horse's neck. "Parker, here, has saved my hide more'n once by refusin' to go into places I wanted. It took us a while to finally understand each other. But now, we know what each other's thinkin'; leastwise, most of the time. After all, if you have to trust your horse, your horse also needs to know he can trust you. *Comprende*, Nate?"

"*Comprende.*"

"Good. Let's get these animals movin'. We don't want the rest of the men to get too far ahead. I'm gonna take down the rope, then bunch 'em up. You stay here, and if any of 'em try to get by you don't let 'em. I doubt any of 'em will. They'd rather stay right here and keep on grazin'.

But if one of them does, you said your horse was a cow-pony, right?"

"Yeah, he was. My brother Jonathan was a cowboy. Big Red was his horse, or at least he was—until Jonathan got killed."

"We'll find those men who killed your folks and our compadres before much longer, Nate. You can bet your hat on that," Phil said. "Meantime, Red'll know what to do. If any of these broncs try'n get past him, just give him his head."

"All right."

Phil untied one end of the rope, gathered it, then untied the other end and hung it from his saddle. As he did, the animals in the *remuda* lifted their heads and pricked their ears sharply forward, watching him.

"I'm goin' in after 'em, Nate. You be ready."

"I will be."

"Good."

Phil rode into the *arroyo* and worked his way behind the *remuda,* bunching the eleven horses and four mules.

"G'wan, get on up there," he shouted, slapping the poppers, which were flat pieces of leather on the ends of his reins, against his leg for emphasis. With tossing of heads and snorts of protest, the animals slowly started out of the *arroyo.* Diablo, the black gelding which had belonged to Ranger Andy Pratt, before he was gunned down by the same men who murdered Nate's family, tried to gallop ahead of the rest and run off.

"Get that black devil, Nate!" Phil shouted.

"Stop him, Red!" Nate pulled Red to the left to head off the racing black. Red broke into a run, cut off Diablo, and slammed into him, shoulder to shoulder. He nipped the black's neck. Diablo stumbled to his knees, regained his footing, and stood, shaking himself off and blowing. Red stayed in front of him, his ears pinned.

"Good job, Nate!" Phil called.

"It was all Red," Nate answered. "He knew what he was doin'."

"Yeah, but you had to start him in the right direction, and let him know what you wanted," Phil said. "You're gonna make a top hand wrangler. With a little seasonin', if you ever quit the Rangers, you'll be able to find a job wranglin' horses on any ranch."

"You mean that?"

"I sure do."

"Then, I'm grateful. Real grateful."

"Speakin' of gettin' practice, let's get this bunch goin'. I'll take the left, you take the right. Stay slightly behind 'em. They may try to run for a bit, but they should settle down right quick."

"I've got it." While Phil shoved the remuda along, Nate worked his way behind them, then crossed to their right side. As Phil had said, for a few minutes the animals loped, but eventually settled into a jogtrot, then slowed to a walk.

"Nate," Phil called, "You'll find out horses and mules have a peckin' order. There's always one or two of 'em which leads the herd. In this bunch we have here, Molly, the big bay mule out front, is the boss. She'll put any of the others who challenge her in their place. When Molly's bein' used, Pete, that chestnut gelding who was Tad Cooper's mount, takes charge. The others all know their places. Now, this ain't really a proper *remuda,* since we've only got eleven horses and four mules in it. On a cattle drive, there'd usually be a lot more mounts. Mebbe only a couple of spare mules for the chuck wagon, though. In fact, that's why we have the extra mules. George'll switch out animals every other day."

"Seems to me these are plenty enough to keep track of,"

Nate answered.

"I reckon you're right," Phil said, with a laugh. "It's also not a bad idea for you to get to know each one by name. Like I just said, the big mule out front is Molly. The other mules are Bonnie, who's right behind her, then Jake and Jill. I don't imagine I'd have to explain to you how to tell Jake and Jill apart."

"I don't reckon," Nate said. A slight smile played across his lips as he recalled the day Jonathan brought Big Red home, and Nate had to ask him whether a gelding was a boy or girl horse.

"Somethin' funny, Nate?" Phil asked.

"Yeah, a bit. You might get a laugh out of this. When Jonathan came home with Red, here, I didn't know the difference. I had to ask Jonathan if Red was a boy or girl."

Phil threw back his head, slapped his leg, and laughed uproariously. By the time he stopped, tears were rolling down his cheeks.

"I'm sorry, Nate. Hope I didn't embarrass you, laughin' so hard. Boy howdy, you were right. That gave me a good laugh. I reckon you can tell a mare from a gelding from a stud horse now, though, huh?"

"I sure can."

"Good. Now, as far as the horses, the palomino, that's the gold-hided horse, is Macy. Behind him, the mouse-colored one, we call that a grulla, is Dakota. Then, followin' behind we have Andy's Diablo, Tad's Pete, Pecos, Bill's Harley, Tex's Waco, Tim's Ramon, Ed's Brazos, Girl, the mare which belonged to that horse thief whose carcass Jeb Rollins and you hauled in, and finally Charcoal, the steel-dust gray."

The horses which belonged to the six murdered Rangers had been added to the remuda. Being a Ranger's horse was almost as dangerous as being a Ranger itself, so spare horses were always needed.

"Good thing that Andy's horse has the white mark down its face," Nate said. "Otherwise, you wouldn't be able to tell him and Carl's Diablo apart. Kind of a coincidence, two black horses in the same outfit, with the same name."

"Not so much as you might think," Phil said. "Diablo means devil in Spanish, as you probably already know. There's lots of horses in these parts named Diablo, and for some reason a lotta men who own a black horse seem to like to call it Diablo.

"Now, as far as that white mark, that's a blaze. If it was just a spot on the forehead, it would be a star. A narrower blaze would be a strip, and a white spot on the nose a snip. White up to the fetlocks, which is kind of a horse's ankles, is a sock. Higher than that it's a stocking. And a cayuse with a mostly white head is called bald-faced, except if it's a white horse, of course. Knowin' all that will come in handy some day, when you're lookin' for some renegade's horse, or some cowboy is describin' his stolen bronc to you.

"There's lots more I can teach you about horse colors and markings. Right now, though, let's get these animals movin' a bit faster. Take your rope off your saddle."

"You mean my lariat?" Nate asked.

"Well, yeah, but don't ever call it that, less'n you want to be taken for a real greenhorn. It ain't a lasso, either. Lasso is what you do with a rope, when you catch somethin' with it. Not that you should ever say you're gonna lasso anythin'. As far as any cowboy is concerned, it's a plain old rope. And you rope a cow. You don't lasso it. Same way, it don't matter whether it's a steer, a bull, a heifer, or a cow. Far as ranchers and cowboys go, when you're roundin' up a herd or drivin' it to Kansas, all cattle are cows."

"Thanks, Phil. That'll help keep me from makin' a fool of myself."

"*Por Nada.* It's nothing. Now, untie the latigo, that's the leather strap holdin' your rope, and take the rope in your left hand. You might have to switch your reins to your right, but you need to hold your rope on the side facin' the remuda."

"All right." Nate untied the rope and lifted it off his saddle.

"Good. Have you ever worked with a rope at all?"

"No, I can't say as I have. I've never even touched this one since I got Red back."

"Then I'll have to start right with the basics, Nate. You see the rope's coiled up. Do you see the little loop at one end, which the rope passes through?"

"Yeah, I see it."

"Good. That's called the honda, although some men call it a hondo. Don't make any difference. That's how you build your loop. You shake out your rope, let as much as you think you need slide through the honda, and start twirlin' your rope right to left, buildin' your loop as big as you need. Then you toss it and catch the critter you want. We're not gonna worry about that quite yet, though. We'll work on ropin' in camp.

"Which reminds me, the first chance you get, buy yourself a pair of good, sturdy, leather gloves. When you've got fifteen hundred pounds of longhorn tied to the other end of your rope and pullin' it through your hands, you sure don't want it burnin' all the skin off your palms. You might want to buy some chaps to protect your legs, too.

"And another thing you never want to say, unless you want to again be taken for a green tenderfoot, is 'chaps'. Chaps is pronounced 'shaps', like it starts with 'sh'. It's short for the Spanish '*chaparejos*'. Mexican vaqueros used them first, then American cowboys adopted them. A good pair of chaps'll protect your legs against the thorny plants we've got all over Texas.

"However, all I want you to do right now is take that rope and slap it against your leg, while talkin' to the horses. Tell 'em to pick up their pace. You can also wave it around, if you'd prefer. Just so those broncs get the idea you want 'em to move faster. Watch how I do it."

Phil took his rope and slapped it against his thigh. "Heeyaw, git up there, you lazy sons of guns. Molly, get 'em movin'. C'mon, git goin'." He urged Parker closer to the remuda, shoving the laggards along.

On his side, Nate swung his rope back and forth. "Step lively there, Red," he urged. "Get Charcoal movin'."

The steeldust was hanging behind the other animals, and drifting off to the right. Nate loped Red up to him. With a nip on the rump, Red chased Charcoal back to the remuda. The steeldust squealed at the sting of Red's teeth, and half-heartedly kicked at him, but resumed his place in the herd.

"Good work, Nate," Phil praised. "Now, let's keep 'em movin'."

• • •

As the sun climbed higher in the sky, it beat down mercilessly on both man and beast. After an hour, Phil and Nate had caught up with the rest of the company. They kept the remuda to its rear, just behind the chuck wagon.

Ordinarily, the wagon would be out front, to keep dust and dirt from settling on the supplies. However, with the danger of attack from outlaws or renegade Indians ever present, Captain Quincy ordered George to stay behind the company, both for his own safety, and to prevent any attackers from shooting and killing the mules pulling the wagon, thus blocking the trail, making the Rangers easy targets, but themselves much harder to hit.

"Better go easy on that water, Nate," Phil cautioned, when Nate took another drink from his canteen. The water it contained was now warm, almost hot, but still soothed Nate's parched throat and lips. "We won't be stoppin' for another couple of hours, and even then there's no promise we'll find water. What you've got might have to last you until tonight, or even sometime tomorrow. You're gonna have to learn how to pace yourself, and drink sparingly."

"I guess you're right. I'm just awful thirsty," Nate said. Nevertheless, he wiped the back of his hand across his mouth, recapped the canteen, and hung it back from his saddlehorn.

A short while later, Phil stood up in his stirrups. He unbuttoned his denims, then turned sideways.

"Phil, what the heck are you doin'?" Nate asked.

"I've gotta pee," Phil explained. "It's a lot easier to pee off your horse while he's movin', rather than stoppin', gettin' down, goin', then gettin' back on and catchin' back up to the others. And you sure don't want to hold up your entire outfit just to stop and pee."

"Seems awful tricky," Nate said.

"Nah, it's not all that hard, once you get the hang of it," Phil said. "The hardest part is keepin' your balance. It's better if you learn to swing your right leg over your horse and just stand in one stirrup, too. A lotta men won't do that. They'll just stand up, turn to one side, and aim as best they can. The problem with that is you usually end up dribblin' down your horse's shoulder... or your own leg. Smarter to do it like this."

Phil swung his right leg over Parker's back and stood with his left foot in the stirrup, bracing himself with his right hand on the saddlehorn to keep his balance.

While his chestnut plodded along, he relieved himself, then when finished swung his leg back over Parker and got his right foot back in the stirrup. He rebuttoned his denims, then settled back in his saddle.

"See, Nate. Nothin' to it."

"As long as you don't fall flat on your face."

"Well, there is that," Phil said. "You sure don't want that to happen if you can help it. Besides the chance of gettin' hurt, it would be downright embarrassin'.

"And by the way, that's another reason to go sparingly on your water when we're on the trail. You won't have to pee so much if you limit your drinkin'. The less intake, the less outflow."

"I get it. And I've gotta agree with you, Phil. Fallin' off my horse while peein' would sure enough be embarrassin', to say the least. In fact, I'd venture it would be downright mortifyin'," Nate answered. "Charcoal!"

Once again, the steeldust had quit the *remuda*. Nate sent Red charging after him.

2

Despite the heat, the Rangers made good time. They reached Menardville shortly after three o'clock. Captain Quincy had hoped to keep their animals in the abandoned Spanish mission compound on the east side of town, which served as a corral for some of the vast cattle herds being driven to market on the north and west trails.

However, the compound, which could hold up to three thousand head, already held a good number of cattle, meaning there was no room for the Rangers' animals. Instead, the captain arranged to set up camp at the north edge of town, on a patch of ground between the livery stable and the San Saba River.

He also made arrangements with Julio Menendez, the stable owner, to put up all the horses and mules in two of his corrals for the night.

Once the animals were groomed, grained and watered, and munching on hay, Quincy gathered his men around him.

"All right, boys, this is the last town you'll see for quite some time," he said. "I'm turnin' you all loose for the night. Buy whatever supplies you think you're gonna need for the next week or ten days. Get yourselves baths, haircuts, shaves, if you want. Have yourselves a good supper, go to one of the saloons for a few drinks, spend some time over a deck of cards or visitin' with a woman, if that's your pleasure.

"Since this'll be your last chance to relax and have fun for the foreseeable future, I'm not settin' a deadline for any of you to be back in camp. The time until sunup tomorrow is yours.

"However, I expect all of you to be on your best behavior. You're in town now, and each and every one of you represents the Rangers, and the state of Texas. You saw all those cows bein' held at the old mission when we rode into town. That many cows means there's a lot of cowboys in town, and where there's a lot of cowboys in off the trail, there's usually a lot of trouble, and we want no part of that.

"So, that means no gettin' drunk, no bein' too rowdy, and no fightin', unless someone else starts it first. And if any of you *do* get so drunk you're not ready and able to ride come first light, you'll have me to answer to. And I *will* make your life miserable, count on that. Is that understood?"

"Perfectly, Cap'n," Lieutenant Bob Berkeley answered. "Are you comin' into town with us?"

"I'll be along in a while," Quincy explained. "I've got a couple of reports I want to finish up, so I can mail them this afternoon. Let the town marshal know we're here, Bob."

"Of course, Cap'n."

"Good. So, unless there are any questions, company dismissed."

"I've got one," George said. "What do you mean, 'good supper', Cap'n? Ain't my grub good enough for you?"

"George, I'm certain I speak for every man here when I say you're the finest camp cook in the Rangers," Quincy answered. "But even *you* can do only so much cookin' off the back of a wagon, with limited supplies. I'm sure you'll appreciate a night off, lettin' someone else do the cookin' and waitin' on *you* for a change."

"Well, as long as you put it that way…"

"Fine, George. Now, as I've already said, company dismissed. Get out of here."

"Yes, sir!" Bob answered. "Boys, let's head for town!"

"We're on our own for the rest of the night, Nate," Hoot shouted, with a whoop. "C'mon, pardner, let's get goin'. We're wastin' time just standin' here."

"I'm just waitin' on you, Hoot," Nate answered.

"Where are you two headed first?" Jeb Rollins asked.

"I don't rightly know," Hoot answered, "But it'll be some place where we can get a good meal. After that, we'll take things as they come. But we've got money to spend, and I plan on doin' just that."

While Nate and Hoot had left most of the reward money they'd earned for capturing the men who held up the San Saba bank on deposit, they had each kept a hundred dollars out to use as needed.

"Hoot, first we've got to find a general store, and mebbe a gunsmith," Nate said. "I need to buy a new rifle to replace mine. Phil also says I need a pair of leather gloves. And, I need some spare duds to replace the ones ruined by that lightning bolt."

"You mind if I come along with you two?" Jeb asked. "I've got to pick up some new shirts and socks myself. Nate, there might be a couple of other things you'll need that I'll think of, too."

"That'd be fine, Jeb," Nate agreed. "I'd like to have you

along to help me pick out a rifle. I still don't know all that much about 'em."

"You know which end is which, and how to hit what you're aimin' at," Hoot said.

"That was more luck than anythin' else," Nate answered. "I still haven't had the chance to practice with a rifle all that much. Let's start walkin'."

Throughout the existence of the Texas Rangers, men in their ranks had come from all walks of life. Surveyors, lawyers, physicians and surgeons, teachers, merchants and shopkeepers, even clergymen had, over the years, been members of the organization.

The Rangers had included, at one time or another, Indians, Mexicans and other men of Spanish descent, and men who had immigrated from most of the countries of Europe. There were men of all faiths, Catholic, Protestant, and Jewish. While most Rangers were young, and single, quite a few were married men with families, and ranged in age up into their sixties.

In Captain Quincy's company, Dan Morton had been a store clerk prior to joining up, and Ken Demarest a railroad conductor. Joe Duffy had ridden shotgun guard for the Butterfield stagecoach line.

However, as held true for the Rangers as a whole, the majority of his men had been cowboys and ranch hands before signing on as Rangers. And, like all cowboys, they hated to walk. Even if traveling only a block, a cowboy would prefer to saddle, bridle, and ride his horse, rather than going on foot.

However, as much as the Rangers hated to walk, they realized a good night's rest, along with a good feed, was crucial for their horses. For the long trek ahead, the animals would be relying solely on the scant grazing and little water available in arid west Texas, until they reached Fort Stockton. So, walk from the stable to town they did. They grumbled, but they walked.

Jeb pointed to a large, carved wooden sign of a revolver hanging over a storefront just ahead. Under it was a smaller sign, proclaiming, "Dale Ferguson, Guns Bought, Sold, and Traded. Repairs of all makes and models."

"There's your gunsmith, Nate," he said. "We might as well stop there first."

"About time," Hoot said. "My feet are killin' me."

"We've only gone five blocks," Nate pointed out.

"Mebbe so, but Texas sure ain't like back East, where you probably walked all over the place, Nate," Hoot answered. "Here, we ride our horses. That's why God gave 'em four feet, and us only two. It's the horses that are supposed to walk, not us."

Nate laughed as they climbed the stairs and went into the shop. It held an array of weapons, in glass cases, on countertops, and in racks along the walls.

A man was seated at a table behind the far back counter. He had a green eyeshade on his head, and a jeweler's loupe fixed over his left eye. On the table was a disassembled pistol.

"I'll be with you in just a moment," he said, putting down the small screwdriver he held. He removed the loupe, shoved back the eyeshade, and stood up.

"I'm sorry to keep you waiting," he said. "I'm Dale Ferguson, the owner of this shop. What can I do for you gents?"

Ferguson was in his mid-fifties, with graying hair and light blue eyes. He held out his hand.

"Jeb Rollins." He and Ferguson shook hands. "My pards are Hoot Harrison and Nate Stewart. Nate's the one shoppin' for a weapon."

Ferguson shook hands with Nate and Hoot, in turn.

"Well, I'm certain I can provide what you need," he said to Nate. "What, in particular, are you searching for?"

"I need to buy a rifle. Mine got blown up when it got hit by lightning."

"*Shocking*," Ferguson said, with a chuckle. "I hope you didn't get too big a *charge* out of that."

"Mister, I'd be careful about keepin' tellin' awful jokes like that with all these weapons around here," Jeb advised, also laughing. "Someone's liable to gut-shoot you one of these days if you do."

"Indeed," Ferguson said. "You probably have a point. Now, down to business. Did you have any particular model in mind, son?"

"Not really," Nate said.

"We're Texas Rangers, on our way to the Big Bend," Jeb explained. "Nate'll need a good, reliable gun. One that can take a beatin' and keep workin', without the loadin' chamber jammin' or the firin' pin breakin'."

"Ah, then I would recommended the Winchester Model 1866." Ferguson took a rifle off the rack behind him and handed it to Nate. "That's a fine weapon, tested over the past few years. It's a real rugged gun. It's also called the Yellowboy, due to the color of the metal forming its receiving chamber. The 1866 is a great improvement over its predecessor, the Henry. As you can see, it's a lever action repeater.

"Nate, I notice you're wearing a Smith and Wesson American, chambered for .44 Henry rimfire cartridges. The Model 1866 takes the same ammunition, so you won't need to purchase two different calibers of bullets if you buy one of those. How does the balance feel?"

"That's the same rifle most of us Rangers carry, Nate," Jeb added.

"Winchester did come out with an updated version, the Model 1873, some time back," Ferguson said. "It's supposed to be even tougher than the Yellowboy. However, the 1873s are still almost impossible to come by. I've managed to get my hands on two of them, and they both sold immediately. I don't know when I'll be able to get any more.

"I can tell you that the 1873 costs quite a bit more than the 1866 you're holding. If I were you, I'd go with that rifle. The design is proven, and I'm certain you'll get years of reliable service from that weapon."

"You don't need to sell me on this Winchester, Mr. Ferguson," Nate said. "It's the same model my brother had, before he got killed. In fact, it was his rifle I was usin' when I got hit by that lightning bolt. I was about to put a bullet in the back of the man who murdered him, and my parents. He's still on the loose. I'll take this rifle, and when I track down that son of Satan, I'll use it to put a bullet through his guts."

"I'm sorry, son," Ferguson said.

"That hombre's gang has killed a lot of other innocent folks, as well as six of our Ranger pards," Hoot added. "They'll have a lot to answer for when we finally do catch up with 'em."

"I can imagine they will," Ferguson said. "Nate, that rifle usually sells for fifty dollars. Since you're a Ranger, I can provide you the twenty per cent discount I offer to all lawmen who purchase a gun from me. That means your cost would be forty dollars. I realize it's a bit steep, but you'll have a good, reliable weapon."

"I'll take it, along with a box of cartridges," Nate answered.

"We have plenty of shells in our supplies, Nate. Don't forget, the state provides those. Texas don't provide anythin' else, except our grub, but she does pay for our bullets. What you do need is gun cleaning supplies, and some gun oil," Jeb advised.

Nate had learned, since being taken on as a provisional Ranger, exactly how low-paying the job was. Ranger privates received only thirty dollars a month and *found*; *found* meaning their food. And out of that thirty dollars, they had to pay for all their supplies, including weapons, clothes, tack, blankets, and provide their own horse, which had to be worth at least a hundred dollars.

The state would reimburse a man if his horse got killed or crippled, but other than that, all expenses above and beyond food and ammunition were the responsibility of the men. It was no wonder recruits were hard to find, and even harder to keep. Risking their lives for less than a dollar a day, bad food, and spending weeks on end in the saddle hardly seemed worth it, to most men.

"I know that," Nate answered, "But I want to make sure I have extra. I will get the other stuff, though. And Mr. Ferguson, I still have the stock from my brother's ruined gun. Somehow, it survived the lightning strike. If I brought that here, would you be able to switch them out?"

"Not right away, I'm afraid. I'm already several days behind on my repair orders. That's why I'm still here so late, trying to catch up."

"Don't worry about that, Nate," Jeb said. "All of us know how to take apart a gun and put it back together. That's one of the lessons you still have to learn, how to clean your weapons. I'll help you change stocks the first chance we get."

"Thanks, Jeb." Nate reached into his pocket and took

31

out several yellowbacks. Ferguson placed a box of cartridges on the counter. He also took a gun cleaning kit and small vial of gun oil from a shelf, and added these to Nate's purchases.

Ferguson took the money from Nate. "Sixty dollars, here. With your discount, it's forty dollars for the rifle. Unfortunately, I can't extend the discount to ammunition or supplies, so it will be another fifty cents for the bullets. The cleaning kit is a dollar, and the oil is forty cents. That makes the total forty-one dollars and ninety cents. Your change comes to eighteen dollars and ten cents. It's been a real pleasure doing business with you."

Ferguson handed Nate the rifle, bullets, supplies, and his change.

"You also, Mr. Ferguson. Thank you."

"You're welcome. And good luck to all of you. Vaya con Dios."

"Adios."

"Where to next, fellers?" Hoot asked, once they were back on the street.

"There's the store, right over there," Jeb said. He pointed to a block-long structure, with a sign that read "Menardville Mercantile" stretching the length of the building. "I'd imagine they'll have everything we need."

• ● •

The threesome spent over an hour in the mercantile. By the time they were finished shopping, Nate had a complete new spare set of clothes, including a bright blue silk neckerchief, as well as two pairs of heavy, leather gloves.

Remembering what Phil had told him, advice Jeb agreed with, he had also purchased chaps to protect his legs from the thorns and needles of the brush and cactus, along with an oilcloth slicker, which would provide protection from the infrequent, but heavy, Texas downpours.

In addition to those that he had also bought a wax-coated bundle of lucifers, matches which were broken off, one at a time, for use. He also got several flints, which Jeb would show him how to use to start a fire without matches. The final items he purchased were a sketch pad, along with several charcoal pencils.

They paused on the boardwalk in front of the store while pondering where to head next. Hoot and Jeb rolled and lit cigarettes.

"Jeb, back at the bank in San Saba, you told Mr. Funston you didn't smoke. So why are you smokin' now?" Nate questioned.

"I don't smoke cigars. Can't stand the smell of 'em," Jeb explained. "But I didn't want to hurt Funston's feelin's by refusin' one of his. It was just easier to tell him I didn't smoke at all. Listen, if you boys don't need me any longer, I see Joe and Ken goin' into the Rooster Tail Saloon down there. I'm gonna join them, long as it's all right with you."

"No, that'll be okay, Jeb," Hoot said.

"It's fine with me. Thanks for all your help," Nate added.

"Don't mention it," Jeb said. "See you back in camp."

"Where do you want to go, Nate?" Hoot asked, as they watched Jeb saunter his way down the road.

"The closest place we can find some food," Nate answered. "We've put off eatin' long enough. I'm plumb starved."

"Boy howdy, I've gotta go along with you there, pardner," Hoot said. "It's been so long since I ate my gut's sunk in so much my belly button is pushin' up against my backbone. Looks like there's a couple restaurants just up the street. We'll pick the one which seems most likely. All right?"

"As long as the food's good and hot, and there's plenty of it, it doesn't matter to me where we eat," Nate replied. "Let's just find a place."

He and Hoot started toward the town's main plaza, which was fronted by the Menardville Hotel and the newly constructed, two-story Menard County Courthouse.

"Boy, somethin' sure smells good, Hoot," Nate said. "Makes my mouth water."

"It must be comin' from that place across the street, just ahead," Hoot answered. He indicated a small building, marked by a sign which read "Chuck's Chuck" in huge red letters. "Let's try it."

He and Nate headed for the little café. They paused to read the lettering painted on its two plate glass windows:

"You'll have good luck if you try Chuck's chuck."

"Spend a buck for real good chuck."

"Tuck into Chuck's Chuck's famous roast duck."

And finally, "Don't get stuck. Eat Chuck's chuck."

"Well, this hombre has a sense of humor, at least," Hoot said.

"Yeah, but not much of one, and he's a real lousy poet," Nate answered. "Let's hope his food is better'n his rhymes."

"Well, the grub *does* smell real good," Hoot said. "Let's take a chance." He pushed open the door and stepped inside, Nate following.

With so many cowboys in town, the place was crowded, but there were still a few seats left. Hoot chose a table in the far back corner. The café was neatly decorated, the tables covered with blue-checked cloths and matching napkins. Flowers in clear glass vases were placed in the center of each table, as well as along the counter. Blue willow patterned plates and various knick-knacks were arranged on shelves. Currier and Ives prints hung on the walls.

"Be right with you fellers," the man behind the counter said.

"We're in no hurry," Hoot called back, as he settled into a chair. Nate took the one opposite.

"Another lesson for you here, Nate," he said. "There was another empty table, and a couple of empty stools at the counter. Why do you suppose I chose this one?"

"I dunno," Nate admitted. "It's closer to the kitchen, so we can get our grub faster?"

"That's a good guess, but not exactly," Hoot answered. "You ain't been a Ranger long enough to know this yet, but we make a lot of enemies."

"Tell me somethin' I don't already know," Nate said. "I figured that out when we got ambushed."

"All right. You never know when a man you had sent to jail for a long time might've gotten out, and is lookin' for revenge. Or, some renegade who's on the Ranger Fugitive List spots you before you spot him."

"The Ranger Fugitive List? What's that?" Nate asked.

"It's a small leather bound book, which contains pages with names and descriptions of men wanted by the Rangers. Every man is supposed to carry one, but right now, Cap'n Dave and Lieutenant Bob have the only copies in our company. If you get a chance to look at one of their copies it'd be a good idea.

"You should try to memorize as much information from the book as you can. We always like to see a page removed from the Fugitive List. It means that man's either been captured, or is dead.

"But, you've got to worry about more than just the men

on that list, Nate. There's always some hombre who just plain don't like lawmen, or wants to make a name for himself by killin' a Ranger. Say he sees you through the window. He'd put a bullet in your back before you even knew what hit you. So, you always want to choose a table against the back wall, with no doors or windows behind you. And you always take a chair that's facin' out. That way, you can see anyone who comes in, and they can't take you by surprise. And with no door or window at your back, you won't catch a bushwhack bullet.

"In fact, you might want to switch chairs right now, pard. Where you're sittin', your back makes a nice, big target for any renegade who comes through that door."

"I see what you're gettin' at, Hoot." Nate shifted his chair to the left side of the table, where he had a good view of the entire room.

"Just don't forget it," Hoot said. "Of course, sometimes you've got no choice but to take another place; but whenever you can, sit where you can see everythin' that's goin' on, and where nobody can get behind you.

"And if you're standin' at the bar in a saloon, make certain to check the back bar mirror every time someone comes through the batwings. You'll stay alive a lot longer that way."

The man from behind the counter approached, brandishing a full pot of coffee, along with two cups and saucers.

"Howdy, fellers," he said. "I'm Chuck. I figured you might want to start off with coffee. Most folks do. And I'm sorry if service is a bit slow. Martha, my waitress, twisted her ankle and had to go home early, to rest it. So I'm both cookin' and servin' tonight."

"The coffee sounds good," Hoot answered. "And we're in

no hurry. I'm Hoot, and my pard, here's, Nate. Pleased to meet you."

"Same here. Don't mind all the geegaws and frillery around the place," Chuck said, as he filled the cups to the brim, then placed the pot on the table. "That's my wife's doin'. I told her all you need to do is serve good grub, and plenty of it, at a fair price, and you don't need to fancy up a place to bring in the customers. But, she insisted I pretty things up to try and get some of the females in town to eat here, also. I get a few, but mostly my trade's with cowboys, ranchers, and farmers. Now, are you ready to try your luck with Chuck's chuck?"

"You can't help yourself, can you?" Nate said, laughing.

"I have to admit I can't," Chuck said. "I try, but I just can't seem to stop."

"That's all right," Nate said. "If your food tastes half as good as it smells, we can put up with the rhymin'."

"That, I can promise you," Chuck answered. "How about a couple of nice, thick steaks, along with fried pota- toes, black-eyed peas, homemade bread with fresh churned butter and molasses, and for dessert two slabs of apple pie?"

"That sounds mighty good to me," Hoot said. "Just don't cook my steak too much. I'd like it so rare it's almost still mooin'."

"Not me," Nate said. "I want mine so done it's almost burnt to a crisp."

"You got it, fellers. Comin' right up." Chuck disap- peared into the kitchen. Hoot took a swallow of his coffee, then leaned back in his chair. He took out the makings, rolled a quirly, and lit it.

"You really oughta try smokin' again, Nate," he said. "You didn't give it much of a chance. And there ain't nothin' which goes quite as good with a fine cup of coffee like this one than a good smoke."

"I'll leave the smokin' to you, thanks just the same, Hoot," Nate said. He also took a gulp of his coffee. "Boy, you're right about the coffee, though. This is one fine brew."

There were two young cowboys, one about Nate's age, the other close to Hoot's, at the table next to theirs, already working on their supper. The older of the pair looked over at Nate and Hoot and gave them a friendly grin.

"Howdy, fellers," he said. "You from around these parts, or are you just passin' through like we are? My name's Matt, by the way. Matt Geyda. My pard's handle is Jonathan Mulero."

"Howdy," Jonathan added.

"Howdy yourselves. I'm Hoot Harrison, and this here's Nate Stewart." Nate nodded. "Yeah, you might say we're passin' through," Hoot continued. "We'll only be in town for tonight. How about you boys?"

"We'll be headin' out first thing in the mornin'," Jonathan answered. "We ride for the Box QL ranch. The spread's about sixty miles south of here. If you rode in from the east, you saw the herd we're drivin' north, bein' held at the old mission. There's two other ranches, the Triangle H and the J Bar J, on the drive with us. We've got a little more than a thousand head, all told."

"We did see 'em," Nate confirmed.

"They were a fine lookin' bunch of cows," Hoot added. "Most longhorns aren't that chunky. They're usually kind of rangy, and tough. Not a lot of meat on 'em. Yours look nice and fat."

"As long as they don't stampede, and run a lot of the fat off 'em, they should bring a good price at the railhead,"

Matt answered. "Hey, you two wouldn't by any chance be lookin' for work, would you? The boss is tryin' to hire on a few more hands. We lost three men crossin' the Llano River. It was in flood, and they got swept away and drowned. We lost about forty head, too."

Hoot shook his head. "Nope, we sure aren't. Nate and I are with a company of Rangers, headin' for the Big Bend country. There's some tall trouble down that way, and we've gotta put a stop to it."

"You two seem awful young to be Rangers," Jonathan said.

"We're older than we look," Hoot replied. "And Nate, here, is still a probationary Ranger. It'll be a while before he's taken on as a regular."

"I needed to sign on with 'em," Nate explained. "I had an older brother, who had the same name as yours, Jonathan. He was a fine cowboy. You would've liked him. We lived with our folks on a small ranch just outside San Saba... until a real bad bunch raided the spread.

"They killed my ma, pa, and Jonathan. They also shot me, and left me for dead. But the Rangers found me, and patched me up. I thought I was gonna have to head back home to Delaware, but things turned out different. Besides, I can't rest until I find the men who murdered my folks. They're still out there, somewhere."

"They've murdered lots of others, besides Nate's family, includin' six of us Rangers," Hoot added. "That's why they've got to be run to ground, as soon as possible, before they kill even more folks. They're a real dangerous outfit."

"Sounds like they're a rough bunch to tangle with," Matt said.

"They are," Hoot agreed, "but us Rangers are tougher. When we catch up to 'em again, they'll find that out."

"Especially that pale-eyed, pasty skinned devil who leads the outfit. I've got a bullet with his name on it. Enough about them for now, though, Hoot. Here comes our supper," Nate said. Chuck was returning, carrying a tray piled high with steaming hot food.

"Here ya go, fellers," he said. "Almost raw steak for you, Hoot, and one charred black for Nate. Plenty of spuds and peas, and a whole loaf of nice, warm bread, along with all the fixin's. Nobody'll ever be able to say they rode away from Chuck's still hungry. I'll bring another pot of coffee soon's you finish that one."

"Thanks, Chuck," Hoot said. He and Nate dug into their food. As Chuck had promised, everything was indeed tasty. The steaks were tender, the potatoes crispy, and the peas fresh from the garden patch behind the café. The bread was soft, and just warm enough so the butter melted into each piece. After they had finished the main portion, Chuck took their plates, then returned with two huge pieces of apple pie, along with yet another pot of coffee.

"Was everything all right, fellers?" he asked.

"Best grub I've had in a coon's age," Hoot answered.

"You mean the best chuck you've had in a month of Sundays," Nate said. "After all, this is Chuck's chuck. And you don't need a lot of pluck to try it."

"Aw, shucks," Chuck said.

"Well, at least no one here's like an old hen. Didn't hear anyone cluck about it," Nate added.

"Will the both of you just stop it?" Hoot said. "Or do I have to shoot the two of you? No jury would ever convict me if I did. Then I'd leave your sorry carcasses lyin' in the muck." He slapped his forehead. "Lord help me, now even I'm doin' it. Chuck, hand over that pie."

"Of course."

Hoot and Nate took seconds on the pie, and finished up with final cups of coffee. Hoot rolled and smoked another quirly.

"I see you've just about finished your supper," Matt said. "We're already done. Either of you have any plans for tonight?"

"Not especially," Nate answered. "We're pullin' out at sunup, so we'll probably just head back to camp and turn in early."

"Before you do, why don't you stick with me and Jonathan for awhile?" Matt suggested. "We can see what else there is to do in this town."

"I dunno," Nate said. "What do you think, Hoot?"

"It's gonna be a long time before we see anythin' resemblin' civilization again," Hoot answered. "I don't see any harm in seein' what this town has to offer. It's still early, so we've got plenty of time to see the sights before we turn in."

"Then that's settled," Jonathan said. "Let's pay ol' Chuck and get on outta here."

• ● •

"Which way do you think we should head?" Jonathan asked, once they left the café.

"It don't matter much, I guess," Hoot answered. "Nate and I don't know any more about Menardville than you fellers." He glanced up and down the street. "Why don't we just mosey our way down toward the saloons? That seems to be where most of the action's at."

"Hold up just a minute, Hoot," Nate said. "You ain't plannin' on gettin' drunk again, are you? I'm not certain I'm ready to feel that bad again. I can still taste how dry my mouth was, and feel the poundin' in my head. Just the

41

thought of takin' a drink has my guts churnin' already."

"Nah, that'd be a real bad idea, especially with all these cowboys in town," Hoot answered. "The last thing we'd need is to get drunk, then get in a fight. That'd get us in Dutch with Cap'n Quincy for certain. I reckon we can wait a spell for our next taste of red-eye. I just want to see what some of the other fellers are up to. It's too soon to turn in."

"Mebbe we can find a dance hall, and try dancin' with some of the girls," Matt suggested.

"You know how to dance?" Hoot asked.

"Nope. He sure doesn't. He can't dance worth a lick," Jonathan answered. "Neither can I. But it seems like it might be fun."

"It sounds like a good idea to me," Nate said. "Heck, I can't dance, and I'd bet ol' Hoot here can't either, but I'd guess those girls could teach us a few steps. And I've heard some of those dance hall girls are awful pretty."

"Those gals at the Dusty Trail back in San Saba had you scared half to death, pard," Hoot said.

"Yeah, but that was different," Nate answered. "We'll just be dancin' here, nothin' else. At least, I don't think so."

"I say let's try it," Matt said. "Can't really hurt nothin', just dancin' with a gal."

The others voiced their agreement.

"Which way do you think the closest dance hall might be?" Jonathan asked.

"Probably the same direction we're headin', down by the saloons and gamblin' parlors," Hoot answered. "Most towns keep places like that in one section, away from the nice part of town. So-called respectable folks don't want places where a man can have a good time too close to 'em."

"Then we'll head that way," Nate said. "We've talked

long enough." He started down the street, with the others hurrying to catch up.

With several outfits in town, spending the night before resuming driving their herds north, the streets were crowded with cowboys and wranglers.

The saloons, gambling dens, dance halls, and other places of entertainment were doing a booming business, packed with men out for a last night of celebration, since the next opportunity could be weeks, or even months, away.

Not wanting to take even the slightest chance of stirring up trouble, Nate, Hoot, and their new found friends gave everyone who crossed their paths a wide berth. There was no telling what the slightest thing might be which would set off a drunken cowboy, and start a fistfight, or worse. Better to be safe than chance getting killed in a gunfight for no good reason, just because a drunk man decided to go for his gun.

They had gone only about two blocks when Nate stopped so short that Matt, who was following close behind, ran right into him.

"Nate, what'd you stop so quick for?" he asked.

"Look!" Nate pointed to the window of the building next to them. A sign hanging just inside proclaimed the establishment as "Gramma Payne's Bakery".

On display were all kinds of cakes, pies, and pastries. But what had caught Nate's eye were several plates piled high with doughnuts, some plain, others dusted with powdered sugar.

"Doughnuts!"

"Yeah, so there's doughnuts," Matt said. "That don't mean you have to stop so sudden-like I nearly broke my nose on the back of your thick skull. Lucky I didn't break any of my teeth. My pa's a dentist, and he sure would've given me what for if I'd come home with a mouthful of busted teeth."

"I'm sorry, Matt," Nate said. His eyes were moist. "But my ma made the best sugared doughnuts in the world. In fact, she fried up a passel of 'em for breakfast the same day those raiders killed her. I can still taste 'em. I hadn't thought about that since, but now that I see these doughnuts here, I've sure got a hankerin' for some. You fellers mind if we stop here first, so I can buy a couple?"

"Not at all," Matt answered.

"I wouldn't mind a doughnut or two myself," Jonathan added.

"Nate, mebbe we can buy enough to take back for the rest of the boys," Hoot suggested. "They'd appreciate that, for certain. Matt, mebbe you and Jonathan can buy some for the other men in your outfits, too."

"That's a good idea," Nate agreed. "In fact, we can buy some for the dance hall gals, too. Some fresh doughnuts might make 'em treat us extra special."

"I dunno," Matt said. "Those gals probably want to keep their slim figgers. They might not want to chance eatin' doughnuts."

"One or two won't hurt 'em," Hoot said.

"Then let's get 'em," Nate said. He opened the door and stepped inside the bakery, with the others right behind him.

"Howdy, boys," the woman behind the counter greeted them. "I'm Maudie Payne, but everyone calls me Gramma. You're in luck. I usually close up shop by three, but with so many men in town I baked extra, and stayed open late, figurin' I'd get some extra business. I have, too. So, what can I do for you fellas?"

44

The bakery owner was in her late fifties. She had gray hair, tied back in a bun, blue eyes, and a friendly smile. Her ample girth indicated she not only enjoyed making her baked goods, but sampling them, too. There was a spot of flour on the tip of her nose, and more flour dusted the red-checked gingham apron she wore.

"We'd like some doughnuts," Nate answered. "How much are they?"

"You're in luck. I just finished making them. Those doughnuts are so fresh they're still warm. And they're only a nickel apiece," Gramma Payne said. "How many do you want? Two or three each?"

"No, more than that," Nate said. "We want to buy some to take back to our partners, also."

"I see. You boys are with one of the trail herds passin' through town?"

"Matt and Jonathan are," Hoot explained. "Nate and I are with a company of Texas Rangers headed for the Big Bend. We're camped for the night behind the livery stable."

"I thought I saw a couple of men wearin' Ranger badges walk by a bit earlier," Gramma said. "Guess I was right. Well, how many doughnuts do you think you'll want?"

"How many are there in the window?" Nate asked.

"I made twelve dozen, and I've sold two of those, so there's ten dozen left."

"We'll take all of those," Nate said.

"All of them?" Gramma echoed. "That a hundred and twenty doughnuts."

"I know that. Matt, Jonathan, how many do you think you'll need? Whatever you don't take, Hoot and I'll keep."

"I figure three dozen should be just about right for us," Jonahan answered. "What do you think, Matt?"

"Sounds good to me," Matt answered.

"That leaves seven dozen for us," Nate said. "Miz Payne..."

"Not Miz Payne... Gramma."

"Gramma, we'll take two each to eat now. If you could wrap up the rest for us, that would be just fine."

"Certainly. That's eighty-four doughnuts for you, so the total is four dollars and twenty cents. For your friends, their total is one dollar and eighty cents. And I'll let you have two sugar cookies each. My treat."

"Thanks, Gramma."

The doughnuts were soon packed in several brown paper bags, which were secured at the top with string. Gramma Payne insisted the boys try one, and a sugar cookie, before she accepted their payment. All four agreed the cookies and doughnuts were the best they'd ever tasted. Nate had to admit they were even a bit better than his mother's.

"If you boys ever pass through Menardville again, you be sure and stop in now," Gramma ordered.

"We sure will. You can count on that," Hoot answered.

"Good. Now don't y'all be eatin' too many of those doughnuts at once," Gramma warned. "You'll give yourselves a real bellyache if you do."

"We won't," Matt assured her. "Muchas gracias, Gramma. Fellers, let's go find those dance hall gals."

• ● •

All four boys were in a jovial mood. They had full bellies, and were looking forward to a few hours in town before their hard work would resume at sunup, Nate and Hoot pushing west with the Rangers, Matt and Jonathan trailing the Box QL herd north for several hundred more miles.

They meandered down the street, watching the passersby, looking into store windows, and munching on doughnuts. Their attention was drawn by a sudden commotion in the middle of the street.

"Get away from us," a woman screamed. "I told you we don't want anything to do with you drunken, uncouth louts." That was followed by a resounding slap across the face of the cowboy accosting her and her companion. There were five others with him.

The two women were young, blonde, in their early twenties, and well-dressed. The face of the one who had slapped the cowboy's cheek was set in furious lines. The other's was flushed with embarrassment.

"Now, honey, that weren't at all nice," the cowboy said. "All we wanted was a little kiss from you and your pretty friend there, and mebbe for y'all to have a little drink with us. Now, we're gonna have to teach you a lesson."

He grabbed the woman and hugged her to him, kissing her roughly. Her struggles against his powerful grip were to no avail.

"Nate, it seems like we're gonna have to take a hand in this," Hoot said. "Otherwise, there's no tellin' what might happen to those gals." Without waiting for a reply, he dropped his sacks of doughnuts and stepped off the walk. When he reached the cowboy, he grabbed him by the shoulder and whirled him around. The surprised man loosened his grip on the woman, and she broke free.

"The lady said she didn't want to be bothered, mister," Hoot said, his voice low and threatening. "So why don't you just leave her alone? You and your friends go back to the saloon and get yourselves some more whiskey. I'm certain you'll be able to find a gal there who's willin' to put up with your pawin' at her."

"This ain't any of your affair, sonny," the cowboy sneered. "If I were you, I'd just back off, before you get hurt. There's six of us, and one of you. Not that it'll take any more'n me to put you in your place."

"I'm makin' in my affair," Hoot said. "As far as the odds, they seem about right."

"That's six of you, and two of us," Nate added, as he, Matt, and Jonathan caught up to Hoot.

"You need a hand, Hoot?" Matt asked. "Jonathan and me are sure willin' to help out. One thing neither of us can stand is a man mistreatin' a female."

"Please, don't start trouble on our account," the younger woman pleaded. "I don't want to see anyone get hurt."

"It ain't no trouble at all to teach yella-bellied skunks like these how to treat a lady," Hoot said.

"Why, you sorry son of a..." With an oath, the first cowboy swung at Hoot's jaw. Hoot ducked the blow, shot a quick right to the cowboy's gut, then was staggered by a punch to his kidneys from one of the man's companions. He went down in a heap, and two men dove after him. They landed in a tangle of arms, legs, and fists.

Two of the other men went after Nate, while each of the remaining two turned on Matt and Jonathan. Matt took a blow directly to his mouth, one to his jaw, another to his stomach, then shot a right to his adversary's nose, crushing it, and bringing forth a stream of blood. He followed that with another punch to the man's left eye, then a return shot to his belly doubled Matt up.

He wrapped his arms around the man's waist and drove him back against a hitch rail. They tumbled over that and onto the boardwalk.

While Matt had his hands full, Jonathan had already

knocked his attacker to the road, with three quick punches to his face. Flat on his back, Jonathan's opponent grabbed the young cowboy's ankle and jerked him off his feet. Jonathan landed on top of him, and they rolled over and over in the dirt, flailing away at each other.

Nate ducked the first punch aimed at him, slammed a fist hard into one cowboy's belly, and when the man jack-knifed drove a knee into his chin. Stunned, the man fell to his face.

The other cowboy who'd gone after Nate hit him in the jaw with a strong left. When Nate staggered back from the impact, he tried to hit Nate in the belly with a hard right. Nate parried the blow, hit the cowboy in the chest, then his chin.

The cowboy countered with two punches of his own, to Nate's left eye and cheek. He tried for Nate's gut again, only to be hit in his own middle by Nate's left fist.

By now, the other man had gotten back up, and he shot a hard right to Nate's ribs. Nate whirled and kneed him in the groin. Howling with pain, the man dropped to his knees. His partner grabbed Nate's shoulder, spun him around, and hit him hard in the middle of his chest. The blow knocked Nate backward into Hoot, who had regained his feet, along with the two men fighting him.

Nate and Hoot fought back to back, trading punches with the four cowboys, blow for blow.

All of them were bloodied and battered now, straining for breath as the punches took their toll. Hoot knocked one man out with a final, vicious punch to the point of his chin. He turned and grinned at Nate, took a punch to his face, then another to his belly. When he jackknifed, he fell straight into a fierce uppercut to his jaw. The blow straightened him up. He staggered back against Nate once again, and when his attacker closed in for the kill, managed to hit him in the throat before he could throw the finishing punch.

Gagging, the cowboy dropped. Hoot kicked him in the belly, then brought his fist down, hard, on the top of his head. He pitched to his face, out cold, all the air gone from his lungs.

Nate had finished off one man with a combination of lefts and rights to the face. He grinned for a minute, as he thought he'd learned his lesson from Jeb, on how to protect his middle, well. Despite the many punches aimed at his belly, not one had landed. He'd managed to block, slide off, or parry them all.

No sooner had Nate thought this than he relaxed his guard, for just a few seconds. Seeing an opening, the other cowboy still standing drove a ferocious punch to the pit of Nate's stomach. Nate folded as the blow knocked him halfway across the street. He landed on his back, rolled over twice, and lay staring up at the sky, struggling to breath. His opponent stood over him, fists clenched, with a wicked grin on his face.

"I've got'cha now, sonny boy," the cowboy sneered. He grabbed Nate's shirtfront and pulled him upright, then drew back his arm, preparing to drive a killing punch to the point of Nate's chin.

Matt and Jonathan had dispatched their opponents, who were both sprawled in the dust, unconscious. Seeing Nate about to have his face smashed in, they raced to his aid.

Before the cowboy's blow could land, Matt hit him in the back, just above his belt. The cowboy arched in pain, his muscles spasming. Matt spun him around and hit him in the gut, folding him into a right to the jaw from

Jonathan. The man dropped like a rock.

The four young men stood, hunched over, blood dripping from their mouths, noses, and chins, as they struggled to draw air into their lungs.

"You all right, Nate?" Hoot asked.

"Yeah. Yeah, I'm okay," Nate answered. He glanced at Matt and Jonathan. "How about you two?"

"I'm fine," Jonathan said. "I've just gotta take a minute and catch my breath. Matt?"

"I'll be okay, pardner," Matt answered. His lips were split open and swollen. He spit out a mouthful of blood, rubbed his jaw, then waggled it, speculatively. "Everythin' seems to be workin'. Didn't break no teeth, either. Good thing. Last thing my pa warned me, before I left home to sign on with the drive, was don't let anythin' happen to my teeth. He'd never let me live it down if anythin' did."

"Not to mention he'd have you in his chair and the drill in your mouth soon as he saw you," Jonathan said, with a slight laugh.

Nate waved at the six cowboys lying sprawled senseless in the dirt.

"Well, at least *we're* in better shape than *they* are," he said, with a chuckle.

"Yeah, but we might not be for long," Hoot answered. "Here comes the marshal. We could be in trouble."

"We could be in even worse trouble," Nate said. "I see Cap'n Dan and Lieutenant Bob comin' right behind him."

Menardville's town marshal, Harry Jones, rushed up. He pushed his way through the crowd which had gathered to watch the brawl. He carried a double-barreled shotgun, which he leveled at the four boys.

"What the devil happened here?" he demanded.

"Lemme handle this," Hoot said. "Marshal, me'n Nate

are Texas Rangers. Those hombres lyin' there were tryin' to force two women to do somethin' against their will. When we tried to help the ladies, they started a fight."

"That's right, Marshal," Nate added. "They didn't leave us any choice."

Captain Quincy and Lieutenant Berkeley had reached Jones' side. They nodded to him.

"What seems to be the problem here, Marshal?" Quincy asked.

"I'm tryin' to get to the bottom of it, Captain," Jones answered. "These here boys yours?"

"Two of 'em are," Quincy confirmed. "The gangly-looking ones to the left, there."

"Well, that confirms part of their story, anyway. They said they were Rangers. They claim those hombres lyin' all over the place, out cold it seems like, attempted to molest a couple of women, and that the fight started when they tried to step in and help the ladies."

"That's the truth, Marshal," the older of the two women who had been the target of the cowboys' unwanted attentions declared. "Those ruffians tried to make us go with them, to dance and…and, well, who knows what else they would have wanted. One of them even forced a kiss on me. Right here in the middle of the street, with everyone watching. It made me feel so dirty." She screwed up her face in distaste. "Heaven only knows what might have happened to us if these boys hadn't stepped in to help."

"Why didn't you say so sooner, Bessie Lou Maynard?" Jones asked. "Do your ma and pa know you and your sister are out, all by yourselves? And you and Jeannie know better than to be out and about on the streets when there are trail herders in town. Cowboys can be mighty rough. Both of you were just askin' for trouble."

"You didn't give me the chance to get a word in, Marshal," she answered. "And how dare you tell me my sister and I can't go to the store, or take a stroll down the street if we like, when there are cowboys in town? Instead of telling us to stay home, as if we were captives, you should do your job, and make the streets safe for decent people to walk. It's not right we should be kept prisoners in our own homes, just because this town allows men to drink, gamble, and do all sorts of other vices to excess, just for the money their evil habits bring in."

"Men have the right to enjoy themselves, Bessie Lou," Jones answered.

"That's right, they do, Marshal," Jeannie spoke up. "I don't have any objection to men having some drinks, doing some gambling, or even…well, as a decent woman I can't say what else, but we all know what goes on at Sonora Sadie's so-called boarding house. Neither does my sister, nor our parents. However, that doesn't give them the right to terrorize decent citizens, who are minding their own business."

"Fine, fine. You ladies have made your point," Jones said. "Captain, since the Maynard sisters confirmed your men's version of what happened, they're free to go. However, I'd advise you to take 'em back to your camp, and keep 'em there until you leave town. That goes for their friends, too. I don't want to see any of 'em in my town again. Reckon we'd better try to rouse these other fellers. Somebody get a bucket of water. Anybody know who they are?"

"They were in my place drinkin', Harry," Burt Hawkins, owner of the Tired Drover Saloon, spoke up. "Said they were with the Double T outfit."

"That's the one which has their herd bedded down just

south of town," Jones said. He turned to one of the by-standers. "Jack, see if the Double T's head honcho is in town anywhere. If not, ride down to where they're camped, and let him know I'll be holdin' six of his men overnight. I'll turn them loose first thing in the mornin', that is, unless you or your sister want to press charges, Bessie Lou."

"No, we don't want to go through all that," Bessie Lou answered. "As long as those men are out of town by morning, that will be sufficient. Jeannie and I would just like to forget this whole unfortunate incident." She turned to the four young men. "And we thank you boys for coming to our rescue. I shudder to think what dreadful things might have happened to us if you hadn't."

"We were just doin' our jobs, ma'am," Hoot said.

"Nonetheless, you were all very gallant, and we're most grateful."

"Hoot, Nate, let's get goin'," Quincy ordered. He turned to Jones.

"Marshal, I'm doing as you requested, for tonight. However, let me point out to you that Hoot and Nate are sworn members of the Texas Rangers. The Rangers' authority, and therefore Hoot and Nate's, supersedes all local and county peace officers' authority. If they decide they need, or want, to return, you will allow them to do so. Understood?"

"Clear as crystal, Captain," Jones answered. The tone of his voice and set of his jaw clearly indicated he wasn't happy with the Captain's statement.

"Good. We'll take our leave now," Quincy said.

"Just one minute, Cap'n," Nate said. "Gotta retrieve our packages." He hurried over to where they had left the sacks of doughnuts, along with Nate's other purchases—including his new rifle—picked them up, and rejoined the others. They began their walk to the edge of town.

"Can't leave these behind," he said. "Hoot and I bought doughnuts for all the men. And I'm sure not gonna forget my new duds and Winchester."

"Fresh doughnuts?" Bob said. "Heck, you could raise all sorts of Cain and not get in trouble, long as you brought back fresh doughnuts."

"Well, I wouldn't quite go that far, but I'm certain the rest of the boys will appreciate those doughnuts," Quincy said. "By the way, who are your two friends?"

"I'm Matt Geyda, and my pard's Jonathan Mulero. We're with the Box QL spread, drivin' a herd north to Kansas," Matt answered.

"Well, I thank you for givin' my men some assistance," Quincy said. "It's appreciated."

"*Por nada*," Jonathan answered. "Like Hoot explained to the marshal, we couldn't let those hombres manhandle those ladies, without tryin' to stop 'em. It's gonna be kinda hard to explain to the rest of the men where we got all these cuts and bruises, though." He rubbed a huge lump rising on his jaw.

"At least I kept all my teeth," Matt repeated.

"Matt's pa's a dentist," Nate explained. "He's afraid if he busts any teeth his dad will bust his butt to go along with 'em."

"Well, once you boys are a bit older, if you'd consider joining up with the Rangers, we'd be glad to have you," Quincy said.

"I dunno. Once I settle down, my pa expects me to follow in his footsteps, become a dentist like him, and help with the business. But chasin' outlaws sure seems a lot more excitin'," Matt said.

Quincy nodded at Hoot and Nate. "Reckon y'all did

exactly what Rangers are supposed to do. Matt, Jonathan, if you come back to camp with us I'll have Jim, our company's medico, fix up your hurts before you head back to your outfit."

"That sounds fine, Captain. *Muchas gracias*," Matt answered.

"Good. We'll be there in a few minutes. Nate, Hoot, once Jim patches you two up I suggest the both of you hit your blankets. We've got a long ride ahead of us tomorrow, and you're both gonna be real stiff and sore. Some extra rest will help; at least, a bit."

"That sounds good to me, Cap'n," Nate said.

"Same here," Hoot added.

"Excellent. I think you've both done enough for one night. Bob and I are pretty tired, too. In fact, we were headed back to camp until we heard of the little ruckus you two stirred up," Quincy said. "It's high time we all turned in."

3

Over the past few weeks, Nate had learned about the dangers of being a Texas Ranger, albeit a probationary one, and the excitement of a Ranger's life. What he hadn't yet experienced was the drudgery of a long, hard trail ride.

He was certainly learning that now. It had been three days since the Rangers had left Menardville, three excruciatingly boring days of their horses trudging over the mainly flat and featureless west Texas plains, and they were still more than three days out of Fort Stockton.

Once the San Saba River, which at this point had shrunk to little more than a good sized creek, veered away from the trail, the trek became truly monotonous. True, there were the occasional *arroyos*, draws, and washes cut into the landscape, and every so often a distant low hill, or flat-topped mesa would pierce the horizon, but for the most part the land was almost table-top level.

The vegetation was also changing the further West the Rangers progressed. Since they'd left the river behind, trees, which had been few enough in number as it were, virtually disappeared. There were infrequent stands of red-berry junipers, some clusters of mesquite grown the size of small trees, and the rare cottonwood, stunted cypress, or pin oak, struggling for life where it had sunk its roots

57

deep, searching for water.

But for the most part, the land's covering was tough grasses, now burned to straw by the heat of summer, and thorny scrub and cactus.

The Rangers' routine was the same each day. Awaken an hour before the sun rose, take care of necessary business and wash up, as best they could, then have a quick breakfast of bacon, beans, and biscuits.

As soon as the meal was finished, camp would be broken, the supplies loaded on the pack mules and in George's wagon. The horses and mules would be brushed and checked for injury or lameness, their feet cleaned out. Then, the horses would be saddled and bridled, two of the mules harnessed to the chuck wagon.

Before the sun was twenty minutes over the eastern horizon, still gilding the morning mist in soft shades of pink, yellow, orange, and rose, the men would be in the saddle and on the move once again.

There would be one or two brief stops to rest the animals; then, around noon, a slightly longer one, when the men would gulp down a quick midday dinner of jerky and hardtack, washed down with tepid water from their canteens. After that short rest, they would head out once again.

There would be one more final, brief stop at mid-afternoon, and then the journey would be resumed. The Rangers would keep traveling until the sun almost touched the western horizon as it set.

At that point, they would find a likely spot to camp for the night. Horses and mules would be cared for before the men saw to their own needs, since their very lives might depend on those animals. A schedule would be set for the sentries, and for the nighthawks who would watch the *remuda.*

After supper, again consisting of bacon, beans, and biscuits, the men would either relax for a short while over cigarettes and final cups of coffee, or would roll out their blankets, pull off their boots and gunbelts, and crawl under the covers, the inky black night sky, stars, and moon for their ceiling, with their saddles for their pillows, and soon fall asleep.

Unless it threatened rain, the tents would remain rolled up, the cots packed away, until the Rangers reached their final destination. The next morning, an hour before sunup, the routine would begin all over again.

Nate was more tired than he had ever been in his life, and had aches in muscles he had never even realized existed. Nonetheless, he never let on how much he was hurting. He'd die before he showed any hint he couldn't keep up with the other Rangers.

This third night out of Menardville, they had come across a small *cienga*, a seep which issued from the base of a low hill. Although it was still an hour before sundown, with a source of sweet water, small though it was, Captain Quincy decided to call an early halt for the night.

After sending Percy Leaping Buck and Hank Glynn to make sure no outlaws or renegade Indians were lying in ambush, they made camp.

Phil Knight wandered up to where Nate was grooming Big Red.

"Hey, Nate," he said. "We've got a little time before supper. That'll finally give me the chance to teach you at least the basics of how to handle a rope. Soon's you're done carin' for your sorrel, grab your rope and follow me."

"Sure thing," Nate answered. He finished brushing his horse, turned him loose with the others, then took his lariat off his saddle.

"Where you headed, Nate?" Hoot asked, when he and Phil walked by where Hoot was rolling out his blankets.

"Phil's gonna teach me how to use a rope," Nate answered.

"This, I've gotta see," Hoot said. "Mind if I tag along?"

"Not at all," Phil answered. With Hoot following, Phil led Nate to a spot at the edge of camp, where the stump of a long-dead juniper stood.

"We're gonna use that stump as your target, Nate," he said. "For tonight, we'll stick with the basics. Later on, I'll show you how to rope from the back of a horse. Eventually, I'll teach you how to catch a movin' target, like a horse, cow, or man. Right now, I'm gonna show you how to shake out a loop, spin your rope, toss it, and catch what you're aimin' for. Does that sound all right?"

"It sounds fine to me, Phil," Nate answered. "And I sure appreciate you takin' the time to teach me."

"Don't mention it. We all had to learn the fine art of ropin' sometime, and someone had to teach us. In my case, it was my pa," Phil said. "You got any questions before we get started?"

"Just one. Hoot said I should have you teach me a couple of different throws. One he mentioned was the Howlin' Man."

"The Howlin' Man?" Phil repeated. Behind him, Hoot was snickering. "I ain't never heard of that throw. Are you certain that's what Hoot called it?"

"Yeah, I'm pretty sure that's what he said. Ain't that it, Hoot?"

"If you say so, pardner," Hoot answered, stifling a laugh.

"I still ain't never heard of a Howlin' Man throw," Phil

insisted.

"Must be the toss where the rope whistles like an Apache when you twirl it," Hoot said.

"Wait a minute. Do you mean the Houlihan, or the Houley Ann, Nate?" Phil asked.

"Yeah. That's the one," Nate said. "I knew it was somethin' like Howlin' Man."

"Good. You had me worried for a minute, thinkin' there was a throw I didn't know of," Phil said. "I can teach you the Houlihan, after a bit. It's a bit tricky, so we'll wait on that until you have the basics down."

"What about the other one? The Johnny's in His Bloomers throw?" Nate asked. "Can you teach me that one, also?"

"What?" Phil exclaimed. This time, Hoot couldn't contain his mirth. He doubled over with laughter.

"Hoot, you were joshin' Nate, weren't you?" Phil asked. "Gave him a couple of funny names for rope throws."

It took Hoot a few minutes to get himself under control, before he could reply.

"No, Phil. I sure didn't give Nate any such name like that. I swear it."

"You mean that ain't it?" Nate asked.

"No, that ain't it," Phil answered. "Think a little harder, will you? See if you can recollect the right name."

"All right." Nate thought for a few moments.

"I've got it. It was the Johnny's Blossoms toss."

Phil just looked at him, dumbfounded. Again, Hoot lost complete control, laughing hysterically while tears rolled down his cheeks.

"You mean the *Johnny Blocker?*" Phil asked.

"Oh. Yeah, I guess that's what I mean," Nate said.

"I sure hope so," Phil said. "I can teach you that one,

too, after you get the hang of a basic throw. Both the Houlihan and Johnny Blocker are underhand throws, where the loop twists before it reaches its target. It takes a lot of practice to be able to pull those off. And if you're smart, you won't let any of the other boys know about those names you came up with. They'll rib you from here six ways to Tuesday."

"Nate might keep his mouth shut, but I sure ain't gonna keep quiet about those," Hoot said. "It'll give me a chance to get even with Nate for spreadin' the story about Dusty dumpin' me on my butt when that longhorn startled him, back outside of San Saba."

"You ain't gonna do that, are you, Hoot?" Nate pleaded.

"A million dollars couldn't keep me from telliin'," Hoot answered. "I can't hardly wait to tell the boys about Johnny havin' pretty posies in his bloomers. Might even have to make up a song about it. Matter of fact, I think I'll just do that. Heck, it might become as famous as *Good-bye, Old Paint* or *The Old Chisholm Trail.* And I'll owe it all to you, Nate."

"Mebbe I'll just crawl under a rock and die," Nate said.

"You don't want to do that," Phil advised. "Most of the rocks around here have snakes, scorpions, horned toads, or lizards under 'em. You don't want to move in on their territory. They can get downright ornery. Well, now that we've all had our laughs, it's time to start your lesson. Watch me, Nate. I'll show you how to start, then you follow my example."

"All right, Phil."

"Here goes. You take your coiled rope in your left hand. Of course, if you were left-handed, you'd do it opposite. You want to keep a length of it, about three feet or so, you'll know what feels comfortable, danglin'. See how I'm doin' it?"

"Yeah."

"Good. You do the same."

Nate shifted his rope from his right to his left hand.

"That looks fine, Nate," Phil said. "Now, you shake out a loop. You let your rope slide through the honda, buildin' the loop as big as you need. I'm gonna build about a three foot circle." He proceeded to do so.

"Now, you start twirlin' the rope, generally over your head. You can make your loop larger while you're doin' that, if you feel the need." Phil began twirling his rope over his head. "Now, you build momentum, all the while keepin' your eye on your target." He twirled the loop faster.

"When you've got the speed you'll require, and you're all set to make your throw, you let the rope go, like so. Then once it's around the target you pull back and tighten the rope." Phil threw his loop, which settled neatly over the stump.

He jerked back on the rope, tightening the loop. "See. Nothin' to it. Nothin' but long hours of practice, and a lot of missed tries and frustration, that is." Phil pulled his rope off the stump and recoiled it. "You wanna give it a try?"

"Might as well." Nate shrugged. "I sure don't want to have to chase another runaway horse or mule without knowin' how to rope."

"Okay. Build your loop, and start swingin' your rope. Soon as it feels right, you try and drop it over that stump."

Nate shook out his loop, then began twirling his rope over his head. After a few swings, the rope collapsed, and settled limply around his shoulders.

"Looks like you done captured yourself there, pardner," Hoot said, laughing.

"You ain't helpin' any, Hoot," Phil scolded. "Nate, start again. This time, snap your wrist more. You need to build more speed. One other thing. When you let go of the rope, you don't so much throw it as just release it. It's the momentum which takes your loop and drops it over your target. Now, try it again."

Nate shook his head, pulled the rope off himself, rebuilt his loop, and swung it again. This time, it spun nicely over his head, until he released the rope. The loop landed three feet to the right of the stump.

"I think you missed, Nate," Hoot said.

"Did you rope whatever you were aimin' for on your first try, Hoot?" Phil asked.

"Well, no. Gotta admit I didn't," Hoot answered.

"Then stop raggin' on Nate, and let him practice. Nate, when you make your toss, you just have to follow through a bit more. Now try it again."

Nate did as ordered, building his loop, twirling it, building up momentum. He let it fly. This time, it missed the stump by a good ten feet to the left. It dropped over Hoot's head and circled his neck. Instinctively, Nate had pulled back when it landed. Hoot started gasping.

"You... you're chokin' me, Nate," he wheezed.

Instantly, Nate loosened his grip. Hoot yanked the loop from around his throat.

"You tryin' to kill me, Nate?"

"Well, that'd be one way to keep you from talkin' about those names I came up with," Nate said.

"Yeah, but chokin' him to death'd make Cap'n Quincy a bit upset," Phil said, chuckling. "However, we do know one thing, now. If we ever have to give a prisoner a rope necktie party, you'll be our hangman, Nate."

"We wouldn't really hang a man without takin' him in

for a trial, would we?" Nate asked.

Phil shrugged. "It's been done. You have to remember, Nate, this isn't the East, where you came from. Things aren't all nice and tidy out here. It can be a long way to the nearest town, even further to one with a jail, and a judge. Sometimes, if a man's guilty, and there's no doubt he is, honest folks have to take the law into their own hands. I'm not sayin' it's right, just that sometimes it's necessary. There's no other choice. You understand what I'm gettin' at?"

"I guess I understand, all right. It just seems kind of harsh," Nate replied.

"It is. But this is a harsh land, son, filled with hard men. That's why us Rangers are out here. We, and other decent folks, are tryin' to make Texas a place where law and order take place of the law of the gun and knife. But I'm afraid it'll be a long time before enough outlaws are cleared out until that happens, if ever.

"Now, enough with the speechifyin'. I never did hanker to be a preacher. Pick up your rope and try again."

It took three more attempts before Nate finally got his rope to settle around the stump. However, he quickly got the hang of timing his release, and the next ten times in a row he roped his target.

"You did just fine, Nate," Phil praised. "Time to call it a night, before your shoulder and wrist are so sore you won't be able to use 'em for a week. Practice whenever you get the chance.

"I do want to point out one thing, just in case you do have to try'n rope somethin' off the back of your horse. Never, and I mean *never*, tie the end of your rope to your saddlehorn. A few cowboys do that, but they're the exception.

"If you latch onto a big, angry as heck longhorn, and he catches you or your horse off balance, he can pull you both right off your feet. If that happens, you'll most likely be crushed by your horse landin' on top of you. And if you ain't, that cow'll use its horns to gore you. A longhorn can gut a horse real easy, so you can imagine what it can do to a man. It makes a bloody mess, that's for certain.

"So what you want to do is, once you've tied onto your target, wrap your rope around your saddlehorn a few turns, real fast. That's called takin' a dally.

"Just remember one thing. Never get your fingers caught between the rope and horn. You'll lose 'em if you do. A lotta men have."

"And a Ranger without a trigger finger ain't no use to the outfit at all," Hoot added.

"Thanks a lot," Nate said.

A spoon banging on a pot got their attention.

"That's suppertime," Phil said.

• • •

Nate slept well that night, dreaming of twirling his rope and making a perfect toss, every time... until an unearthly chorus jerked him awake. He yelled, and reached for his six-gun.

"What're you screamin' about, Nate?" Jim Kelly asked.

"What's makin' that infernal racket?" Nate said, his voice shaking slightly. "Sounds like Satan and his minions, come to get us."

"Those? Those are just coyotes," Jim answered. The howling had now quieted to a few yips. "You mean you ain't never heard a coyote singin' before?"

"I dunno if I'd call that singin', but no," Nate said. "What're they carryin' on about?"

"Can't tell," Jim said, as the howling started again, soon reaching a pitched crescendo. "Might've made a kill, might be tellin' each other where they are, or might be howlin' just to howl. It don't matter why. They ain't gonna hurt you. Now, get back to sleep, and let the rest of us get our shut-eye."

"Okay," Nate said. He laid back down, and, despite the ringing of the coyotes' howling in his ears, soon was sleeping once again. All too soon, George was shaking his shoulder.

"Time to make breakfast, Nate," he said. Nate tossed off his blankets and sat up, with a groan. Someday, he'd be a full member of the Rangers. Until then, he was still a camp helper, and George depended on him to help gather firewood, make the meals, and clean up.

Nate didn't mind, but sometimes he wished he could get the extra hour of sleep the other men got. He pulled on his boots, hat, and gunbelt, stood up, and stumbled toward the chuck wagon.

• • •

Percy Leaping Buck approached Captain Quincy while they were eating breakfast.

"Good mornin', Cap'n," he said. "Looks like it's gonna be a fine day."

"It does seem so," Quincy agreed. "You have somethin' on your mind, Percy?"

"Yes, I do. With your permission, I'd like to scout ahead for a bit, beginnin' today. We're starting to get into territory where there's liable to be a few bands of renegade Apaches or Comanches roamin' about, mebbe some white renegades, or even some Mexican outlaws who have slipped across the border. It'd be a lot easier for one man to spot 'em, without being seen by them, than a whole company of Rangers. And with any luck, I'll be able to bring down a pronghorn or two. All the men are tired of bacon, beans, and nothin' else to eat. They're ready for fresh meat. I know I certainly am."

"That's a good idea, Percy. I do have one favor to ask of you, however."

"Of course. What is it, Cap'n?"

"If you wouldn't mind, take Nate along with you. He needs some more lessons in trackin', and in scoutin' out sign. I'm pretty certain he's never hunted, either. Since you're one of the best men in the company with a long gun, you can teach him how to hunt."

"I guess that will be okay," Percy said. "Nate's still mighty green, but he's handled everything we've thrown at him, so far."

"Good. As long as you're out there, you might as well find us a place to stop for the night. We'll catch up to you. Just be careful, Percy."

"I always am, Cap'n. And I'll take good care of the boy."

"I know you will. You might as well get started. Nate!"

Nate looked up from where he was gathering dishes from the wreck pan to wash.

"You called me, Cap'n?"

"Yes, I did. Percy is going to do some scouting ahead of us today. He's also going to try and hunt down some game. I want you to go with him. You can learn a lot from Percy, so I need you to pay close attention to whatever he tells you. Go saddle up."

"All right, Cap'n." Nate dropped the tin plates he held, with a clatter. Even with his limited experience, he knew riding out ahead of the company might be fraught with danger. Outlaws or Indians would be far more likely to attack one or two men than an entire company of Texas Rangers. But, by now, Nate would rather face a whole bunch of desperadoes, or an entire tribe of Indians on the warpath, than wash one more dish. Not even hesitating, he headed for his horse.

• • •

Percy and Nate rode well ahead of the Ranger company. Percy was dressed in leggings, buckskin moccasins, and an open leather vest, with no shirt underneath. His black hair was long, hanging over his shoulders. He was mounted on a long-legged pinto mustang. The horse was almost all white, except for two buckskin patches on his flanks, and a buckskin "hat" covering the top of his head, and both his ears. The gelding's only other marking was a buckskin spot on his nose.

"Those are pretty unusual markings on your horse, Percy," Nate said.

"They are indeed," Percy agreed. "Markings like Wind Runner's, here, are extremely rare. Us Indians call them Medicine Hat markings, and horses who have them, Medicine Hat horses. They're supposed to bring their riders good luck, especially in battle. I've never held with that superstition, however. I've seen many a bullet or arrow go right through a man riding a Medicine Hat horse as easily as one riding a bay, sorrel, or what-have-you."

He patted his horse's shoulder. "This ol' fella's a brave one, and tough. He's gotten me out of many a tight spot. That's a fine looking animal you have, also."

"Thanks, Percy. I can't claim credit for pickin' him out, though. He was my brother's horse."

"I know that. And as long as you are riding his horse, your brother will be riding with you. That, I do believe."

"*Muchas gracias.*"

"I see you're picking up a little Spanish, Nate," Percy said. "That's good. You really need to know the language out here."

"I've found that out," Nate answered. "You mind if I ask you another question?"

"Go right ahead. If I find it offensive, or one I don't wish to answer, I'll let you know."

"Okay. I always thought Indians couldn't speak English, or at least not very well, even if they did learn a few words. You speak it better than most of the other men. Where'd you learn how to speak it so well?"

"I was fortunate. I befriended a Jesuit missionary priest, Father Thomas Croteau, back in east Texas. He arranged for me to attend the *College of the Immaculate Conception in New Orleans. I not only speak English, but also Latin, Greek, French, Hebrew, and of course Spanish. You're riding with one highly educated Tonkawa, son."

"I reckon," Nate said, shaking his head in wonder. "I have to admit, I've never heard of an Indian who went to college."

"There are more of us than folks know. For example, Dartmouth College, up in New Hampshire, was first established to educate Indians. Unlike a lot of white men think, most Indians, and black men, for that matter, are just as intelligent as any white."

"Or as dumb," Nate said.

"You're certainly correct about that, too."

"Can I ask just one more question?"

"Why not? We've got all day."

"Why are you helpin' the Rangers?"

"That's a long story, which goes way back in my people's history," Percy said, with a slightly bitter laugh. "I'll shorten it up for you. Us Tonkawas have always had plenty of enemies we've had to deal with. There were the Apaches, Comanches, and Karankawas. The Karankawas were probably the worst. They were a really fierce tribe, and practiced cannibalism. Of course, I have to admit, some of us Tonks did also. We believed if you ate a part of your slain enemy some of his strength, courage, and spirit would be passed on to you."

Percy looked at Nate and grinned.

"Hey, don't look at me thataway, Percy," Nate said.

"Don't worry. I wouldn't eat your heart or liver... at least not yet," Percy answered. "You're still a bit too young to have the warrior's spirit."

"That's a real comforting thought," Nate said. "You're just waitin' for me to fatten up, like a turkey or steer."

"Then just stay skinny, and you won't have to worry," Percy said, with a laugh. "Anyway, to continue, for us to survive, since we were a smaller nation than many of the others, we often were forced to make alliances. We were pushed off the plains and into Texas by the Apache. Luckily for us, we didn't subsist only on buffalo and other game, although they were our main source of food, clothing, and housing.

"Unlike most Indians, we also eat fish and oysters. But there was a lot of hunger caused us by the Apaches. When the Comanches arrived, we made an alliance with them, against the Apaches. Later, things turned bad between us and the Comanches, so some of our members realigned themselves with the Apaches.

"And while all this was going on, the Spanish arrived. We never had good relations with them. In 1758, we joined the Apaches and some other tribes in destroying their mission at San Saba. Years later, we did reach an uneasy truce with the Spanish. However, we never really had a cordial, trusting relationship with them."

"So why are you helping whites now, Percy?"

"It all goes back to our need for allies, and for the way the Anglos treated us when they first arrived. We always got along with your people. They helped us fight the Comanches.

"The Rangers, in particular, wiped out what was left of the Karankawas, so we were, of course, grateful for that. We've worked with the Rangers since that time. And we remained friends with the whites, even though, in the late 1850s, some of them attacked the reservation Texas set up for us along the Brazos, and killed many Tonkawas. In 1859, those who were left were taken to a reservation up in the Territories.

"During the War, with no soldiers to protect us, we were attacked by a number of other tribes. By then, there were only about three hundred of us left, and about half were killed in the raid. The survivors worked their way back into Texas, and settled just outside Fort Griffin. Quite a few of us now serve as scouts for the United States Cavalry. Others, like myself, ride with the Rangers. However, our numbers are dwindling, and I would expect in the not-too-distant future, the Tonkawa people will disappear, just like the Karankawas and so many other tribes."

"And yet you still help us. You're a better man than most, Percy."

"Not particularly. I just do what I have to do to survive. And speaking of surviving, we'd better stop talkin' and start lookin' for some game."

"All right."

As they rode along, Percy pointed out different features of the land, as well as plants which could be used for food or medicine. Nate had never realized so many plants, which to him looked mostly like weeds, could provide life-giving fluids, food, or medicine. He'd never have imagined jelly could be made from the fruit of the prickly pear, or a medicinal tea from the manzanilla plant.

"Do you see the thin line of greenery off to the left there, Nate?" Percy asked, some time later. "It's at the base of that low mesa."

"Yeah, I do. Is there anything special about it?"

"That means there's some moisture, probably a spring or even a small waterhole. And where there's water, there's usually game to be found. We'll ride over that way and see what we can scare up."

"Okay." They turned their horses off the trail. Different birds and animals scattered before their approach.

"Those fast, skinny birds are roadrunners," Percy explained. "They run real fast, and like to eat snakes, especially sidewinders. They also eat a lot of bugs. Now, those plump ones hidin' under that prickly pear are prairie chickens. They're mighty good eatin', and I'd ordinarily try to shoot a mess of 'em, but I want to see if we can find an antelope first."

"You've got really good eyes, Percy," Nate said. "I didn't see those until you pointed 'em out."

"It's just a matter of training your mind, and eyes, to observe everythin' around you."

"What the devil is that?" Nate exclaimed, pointing at an ungainly, armored animal which emerged from the brush and crossed in front of them.

"That? That critter's an armadillo. It ain't good for much, except diggin' up termite and ant hills. And mebbe for a laugh."

"A lotta the critters out here are pretty strange-lookin',"

Nate said. "Even the rabbits."

Several jackrabbits had burst from the brush and scattered in front of their horses. However, one remained frozen in place, about sixty or seventy feet ahead.

"Nate, that fella's just askin' to be our dinner," Percy said. "You want to try for your first game kill? Move slow and easy, and don't make a sound, or you'll spook him."

Nate hesitated, then slowly lifted his gun from its holster. He took careful aim at the rabbit's head, thumbed back the hammer, and pulled the trigger. His shot took the rabbit cleanly, right between its long ears.

"Good shot, Nate!" Percy said. "We'll clean and cook him, once we get under those trees."

They rode up to the dead rabbit. Nate began to dismount to retrieve it, when a distinctive buzzing came to his ear. Big Red reared, nearly throwing his rider. Percy yanked out his pistol and fired one shot. The bullet took off the head of a four-foot long diamondback rattlesnake. Red stood, snorting and quivering. Sweat broke out on Nate's brow, and he felt shaky inside.

"Well, now we know what had the rabbit mesmerized, Nate," Percy said, as he punched the empty cartridge from his gun, replaced it, and slid the gun back in its holster. "He was about to be that snake's meal, instead of ours. Well, we eat even better, pardner. You get the rabbit, while I get the snake."

"We're gonna eat snake?" Nate asked.

"Sure. It's good eatin'. And sometimes it's the *only* eatin'."

"Long as you say so."

They dismounted, retrieved the carcasses, then remounted and finished riding the rest of the way to the mesa's base. What Percy had described as trees were mainly scrub willow, mesquite, and stunted cottonwoods, surrounding a decent-sized waterhole.

"See those willows? You can use their bark for tea, or make up a poultice with it. They're good for easin' pain. Well, there's no game here, but at least there's wood for a fire, and fresh water," Percy said. "We'll let our horses drink, then you gather some wood and start the fire while I gut and spit these animals."

"All right.

There were plenty of dead branches lying on the ground, so it only took Nate a few minutes to gather enough for a good sized blaze. Percy waited to clean the rabbit and snake until he could show Nate how that was done. In a short while, the meat was skewered on a spit and roasting over the fire, grease crackling and flaring when it dripped into the flames. Soon, Percy was pulling chunks of meat off the spit.

"You want to try rabbit or snake first, Nate?"

"I'm gonna hold my nose and try the snake."

"Good for you." Percy passed a piece of the diamond-back to him. Nate hesitated, then shoved it in his mouth. The meat was tough and chewy, but palatable.

"It tastes like..." he began.

"Don't tell me. Chicken," Percy said.

"Nope. It tastes like snake."

"Well, at least the rabbit will taste like rabbit."

Eager to get on the trail again, they made short work of the meager meal. The fire was put out, the cinches retightened on the horses and the bridles put back in place. They were getting ready to remount when Wind Runner lifted his head, pricked his ears sharply forward, sniffed the air, and snorted.

"Riders comin'," Percy said. "We'd best see who it is.

You stay here, Nate, and keep the horses quiet. Can't chance them callin' to those other cayuses and givin' us away. I'll take a look."

"All right." Nate took the horses' reins and clamped his hands over their muzzles, while Percy dropped to his belly and crawled into the brush, moving almost silently. He reappeared only a few minutes later.

"Comanches!" he whispered. "Must be a bunch who jumped the reservation. There's six of 'em, and they're headed for the water, right at us. We've gotta be ready for 'em."

"You think mebbe they won't spot us?" Nate asked.

"They're Comanches. They already know we're here. We'll have to fight them off."

Nate's blood ran cold, and a lump rose in his throat. A solid block of ice seemed to settle in his stomach. For one brief moment, his mind flashed back to when his friends in Delaware had heard he was moving to Texas. All they could talk about was he'd have the chance to fight Indians, and how much excitement that would be.

Well, right now, he fervently wished he could trade places with his friends. They could have the excitement and danger—as well as the lance, which would most likely puncture his gut, before this day was done.

"Nate?" Percy's voice, low and anxious, snapped him back to the present.

"Yeah, Percy?"

"There's quite a few boulders scattered at the base of the mesa. Our only chance is to hole up behind 'em. They'll provide decent cover, and with any luck we can hold off the Comanch' until the rest of the men catch up to us."

"We rode off the trail, remember?"

"Yeah, but you can be certain the boys will see our

horses' hoof prints. Not to mention, they'll hear the gunfire and see the powder smoke. Now let's get movin'. We don't have much time. Let's just hope there's no quicksand on the other side of this waterhole to bog us down. Let's go. And don't worry about bein' seen. They might know we're here, but those Comanch' won't be expectin' us to make a move, not quite yet. Just stay low over your horse until we get behind those rocks."

"Okay, Percy. You've fought Indians, and I haven't, so I'll do whatever you say."

"You mean *other* Indians," Percy said, grinning. "Don't forget, I'm also an Indian. Let's move, now!"

The two Rangers sprang into their saddles, drummed their heels into their horses' ribs, and sent them splashing through the water and across the muddy ground on the opposite side.

Big Red stumbled in the middle of the muck and nearly went down, but Nate's firm hand on the reins pulled his head back up, steadied him, and got him moving again.

Behind them, the Comanches, seeing their prey, whooped and hollered, and sent a few rifle shots in their direction.

Nate and Percy raced their horses into the shelter of the rocks, grabbed their rifles from their boots and spare ammunition from their saddlebags, and led the mounts behind the largest of the rocks, where they would be safe from any bullets or arrows, except a chance ricochet. Nate and Percy bellied down behind adjacent rocks.

"How do you think they'll come after us, Percy?" Nate asked.

"Dunno for certain. We're in pretty good shape here. They might try to circle around, but there's not all that much room for 'em to maneuver. They could try to wait us out, or hold out until dark when they can sneak up on us. But I'd imagine they'll try to rush us, at least once. When they do, be ready for 'em. Don't fire too quick, though. Make sure you have a good target. We can't waste any bullets. If we can get two of three of those Comanch', the others might decide it ain't worth comin' after us."

The minutes ticked slowly by, five, ten, fifteen. Nate pulled off his Stetson, wiped sweat from his brow, ran a hand through his soaked hair, and set the hat back in place.

"When're they gonna make their move?"

"That's part of their plan. They're waitin', hopin' to see if we break first. Just hold on a few more minutes, Nate. They'll be attackin' any time now."

Nate's heart was pounding, his every muscle tense. Sweat soaked the back of his shirt, made dark circles under his arms, and trickled down his chest. Biting flies and other insects tormented him. When he raised up, just for a moment, to slap at one, a bullet smacked into his sheltering rock, just below him, then ricocheted away.

"You'd better stay down, no matter how much those bugs bother you, Nate," Percy cautioned. "A bullet bites a lot harder'n any horse fly or skeeter."

Nate nodded a silent reply, then settled back to wait. He had his rifle laying on the top of his boulder, ready to shoot the minute an Indian came into range. Just when he thought he could bear the tension no more, they came, galloping their horses out of the brush and through the water, whooping and hollering.

"Let 'em get a bit closer, Nate," Percy urged. "Now!"

He and Nate fired at the same moment. Two of the Indians went down, knocked off their horses and into the water with bullets in their chests. They levered and fired again. Blood spurted from a third Indian's stomach, where Percy's shot hit him. Nate's bullet hit low, striking the ground in front of his target's horse.

All four of the remaining Comanches, the wounded man slumped over his horse's neck, spun their mounts and raced back into the brush. Percy and Nate hastily re-loaded their rifles.

"Think they turned tail and ran?" Nate asked.

"Comanches? Not a chance," Percy answered. "They'll be back. Now, it's also a matter of pride, since we killed two of their companions, probably three. That means they have to kill us, to save face. And hey, aim a little higher, will ya? You've got to remember the farther a bullet travels, the more it drops. That's why your last shot missed so badly."

"All right," Nate said. "Sure wish I had my canteen. I'm dyin' of thirst."

"You chance goin' after it and you'll be dyin' from a bullet or arrow in your back, instead," Percy pointed out. "You'll just have to make the best of it. Put a pebble in your mouth if it's so dry. That'll help some."

"You sure? All right, I'll try it." Nate picked up a pebble lying at his feet, rubbed it clean on his shirtsleeve, then popped it in his mouth. To his surprise, it did slake his thirst, at least a bit.

For close to an hour, the two sides maintained a stand-off. Having lost three of their number, at least two of them dead, the Comanches were wary, realizing a full frontal charge would be futile. Nate and Percy were effectively pinned down.

The one time Percy attempted to shift position, a bullet and arrow which came far too close for comfort convinced him he'd be hugging that boulder until the fight was over, one way or the other.

"I sure hope Cap'n Quincy and the men find us soon," Nate said.

"So do I," Percy answered. "I kinda figured they'd be here by now. And these hombres have gotten awful quiet, even for Comanches. I figure they're up to somethin'. Keep your eyes peeled."

"All right." Nate didn't need to tell Percy how hard it was to keep his eyes peeled. Between the blinding sun reflecting off the ochre hued rocks, the sweat dripping into his eyes, and the strain of staring across the waterhole, searching for their enemies, he was constantly fighting to keep his vision from blurring. He'd just run the back of a hand across his eyes to clear them yet again when Percy shouted a warning.

"Here they come, Nate!" A bullet ricocheted away from the cliff behind Nate, and an arrow bounced off the rock in front of him. Patiently, the Comanches had worked their way around the waterhole, and were now attacking from each side.

Nate emptied his rifle at the two men racing at him, their zigzagging paths, ducking and rolling making them almost impossible to hit.

He yanked out his American just before the two reached him, and fired. Blood blossomed on one Indian's chest, and he tumbled to the ground. The other lunged for Nate, grabbed his wrist, and pulled him onto his back, knocking the pistol out of his grasp.

Both sprang to their feet, the Comanche with a knife in his hand. He swung the razor-sharp weapon at Nate, who sidestepped just enough to avoid the fearsome blade being sunk deep into his gut.

Instinctively, he reached for his own knife, and pulled

the heavy Bowie from its sheath. The Comanche glared at him, his dark eyes glittering with hate. He began waving his knife, muttering in the guttural Comanche tongue.

As the Comanche waved his knife, circling and stalking, Nate forgot everything Hoot had taught him about knife fighting. Instead of maneuvering, trying to circle and dodge the Comanche's weapon, he froze. Stock-still, he stared at the Indian's bone knife, the blade almost white as new-fallen snow, his nerves tight, unable to make his muscles follow his brain's commands.

He barely reacted in time when the Indian lunged at him. Somehow, he twisted just enough so the Comanche's blade slid along one of his ribs. As it did, Nate brought his knife up and into the Comanche's belly. He was surprised at how easily the Bowie's thick blade sliced through flesh and muscle, to bury itself to the hilt.

Hot blood splattered over Nate's hand. As the Indian fell, Nate dropped to his hands and knees and vomited. He turned at the sound of one final gunshot. The Comanche who had gone after Percy lay crumpled at his feet.

"Nate! You all right?" Percy asked.

"Yeah. Yeah, I'm okay. Just kinda sick to my stomach, is all. How about you?"

"I'm fine. Looks like we get to keep our scalps another day, pardner. But you're hurt more'n just a queasy belly. Better let me take a look at you."

"Huh?" Nate glanced at the ripped and blood-soaked side of his shirt. Suddenly, with the fear and excitement of the fight over, he felt a burning along his ribs. He'd never even realized he'd been wounded.

"Lean back against that rock, so I can check you over," Percy ordered. When Nate complied, Percy opened his shirt, then whistled.

"No wonder you got sick to your stomach, kid. That brave nearly sliced open your brisket. You wait here. I'll get bandages from the saddlebags."

"You really think I'm goin' anywhere?" Nate answered, with a thin smile.

"No, I reckon not," Percy said. "You take it easy. I'm gonna gather some willow shoots and bark for a poultice to put on that wound. Be back quick as I can."

"Percy?"

"Yeah, Nate?"

"It ain't the cut which made me sick. It was that Comanche's insides splatterin' all over me."

"Don't worry about it," Percy said. "That'd be enough to make any man sick, even a hardened veteran. You'll get over it."

"Thanks, Percy. I appreciate that."

"Never mind. Like I said, you just take it easy while I boil up those shoots and bark."

Exhausted, Nate dozed off while Percy gathered the willow shoots, as well as some moss, and the bandages.

"Sorry to wake you up, kid," Percy said, when he returned, "But that cut is still bleedin' some. I've got to get that stopped. This moss'll due the trick." He wadded a good portion of the moss, and packed it into the slice along Nate's rib. "There. That'll hold you while I make the poultice."

"Good thing my name ain't Stone, and I ain't movin' much, rollin' around," Nate said.

"What d'ya mean by that?" Percy asked.

"Because we all know a rolling stone gathers no moss. You wouldn't be able to keep that stuff in there," Nate deadpanned.

"You're hurt worse'n I thought, Nate," Percy retorted,

chuckling despite himself. "Be back in a few minutes."

"Wait, before you go…"

"What is it, Nate?"

"You ain't gonna eat any of those Comanches in front of me, are you, Percy?"

"No, I sure ain't," Percy assured him. "Unlike some of my ancestors, I never had any desire to sample human flesh."

"That's good," Nate said. "Because I could see handlin' a turkey drumstick, but a man's leg as a drumstick? That'd be one big hunk of meat. Way too much for me to finish."

"Now I know you're hallucinatin'," Percy said, laughing. "Just try'n rest."

Besides making the poultice, Percy boiled up a medicinal tea from the willow shoots. "This'll help with the pain, a little," he said, as he gave a tin mug full of the brew to Nate. While Nate sipped at the tea, Percy plastered the poultice over his wound, then tied a bandage around his middle, to hold it in place. He had just finished when three evenly spaced gunshots rang out, followed by a shout.

"Percy! Nate! Where are you two?"

Percy clambered to the top of a boulder and waved his arms over his head.

"We're back here, Cap'n. It's sure a relief to see you boys. Ride on in."

A few minutes later, the entire company splashed their horses through the water and rode up.

"About time you showed up," Percy said. "We could have used a little help around here."

"I can see that," Quincy answered. "Looks like you had a bit of trouble. Nate, how bad you hurt?"

"He'll be okay, Cap'n," Percy replied. "Just got a knife

slice across his ribs. The Comanch' who tried to stick him is in far worse shape. Nate gutted him clean. As far as us havin' a bit of trouble, that's an understatement, to say the least. There was six of those Comanch', and two of us."

"You killed 'em all?" Jeb Rollins asked.

"I believe so, Jeb. Only one rode away, but he had my bullet in his stomach. I doubt he got far. Where in the world were you boys?"

"We got sent on a wild goose chase by some rancher who waved us down, claimin' a bunch of his cattle had been rustled," Quincy explained. "Turns out they'd just wandered off into a draw. But it cost us some time, and apparently, almost cost yours and Nate's lives."

"Nothin' to be done for it now, Cap'n," Percy said.

"Joe, Dakota, Carl, Lee. Take the bodies of those Comanches and drag 'em into the brush. There should be six," Quincy ordered.

"Right away, Cap'n," Dakota answered.

"Cap'n, we never did come across any pronghorns, so there won't be any fresh meat for supper," Percy said. "I apologize for that. But we did find you a right nice campsite."

"And just where might that be, Percy?"

"Right here, Cap'n. We're gonna spend the night right here."

• ● •

After supper, Percy and Jim rechecked Nate's wound. Jim decided against stitching it. Both men declared he would be fit to ride come morning. He would be sore, but he'd be able to stay on a horse.

Nate drifted off to sleep with Hoot sitting alongside him, keeping vigil over his injured friend and partner. The other

Rangers, except for Larry and Shorty, who were on the first watch, had gathered around the campfire while Percy regaled them with the tale of the pitched battle with the Comanches.

"Boys," he concluded, "I know Nate's still too young to be taken into the Rangers as a regular. And he still makes rookie mistakes. Gets scared, too, as any man with half a brain would, let alone a kid like Nate. But he's as brave a man as I've ever fought alongside, and has more guts than most. He even sampled a rattlesnake I shot... one which came closer to sinkin' its fangs into Nate's leg than he realized. I'd take him as my pardner any day of the week."

4

The next morning, despite his injury, Nate was back in the saddle again. He was offered the chance to ride in the back of the chuck wagon by Captain Quincy, but declined. If he was going to make it as a Ranger, he'd have to tough out even worse wounds than the knife cut along his side.

Once he settled on Big Red's back, the pulling and soreness of the wound didn't bother him all that badly. Percy's willow shoot and bark poultice had clearly done its work well. By the time the Rangers had ridden an hour, Nate's pain had subsided to a dull ache, not much worse than a bad sprain or bruise.

As Captain Quincy and his men worked their way westward over the next three days, the terrain steadily got more rugged. The level plain gradually became more rolling, broken more often by canyons, *arroyos*, and draws.

Flat-topped mesas and low hills also became more frequent. The vegetation became more sparse, even the few trees which had previously dotted the land virtually disappearing, to be replaced by tough grasses, mesquite, thick, thorny brush, oily creosote bushes, and all sorts of cacti.

The elevation steadily increased, too, so that no matter how blistering hot the temperature became during the day, it often plunged forty degrees or more at night.

After having roasted under the desert sun all day long, the men had to slide under their blankets at night to keep warm.

What was hardest on the men, horses, and mules, however, wasn't the blazing hot sun, the harsh chill at night, the lack of shade, or the shortage of water. It was the omnipresent dust.

The soil became sandier the further west they rode. It was dry as powder, so the horses' and mules' hooves and chuck wagon's wheels kicked up clouds of thick, blinding, choking dust; dust that found its way into every opening in a man's clothing, alkali dust that burned a man's eyes, that clogged his nose and ears, that filled his mouth like cotton.

Dust, that seemed to seep deep into every pore. Dust that coated the horses and mules, so that even the darkest bay or black soon resembled a light brown pony.

And even the slightest breeze, which ordinarily would have provided welcome relief from the heat, instead added to the Rangers' misery, as it stirred up even more dust, stinging every bit of exposed flesh, making it even more difficult to breathe. The men had lifted their bandannas to cover their mouths and noses, so that they looked more like a band of outlaws than a company of Texas Rangers.

They had taken spare bandannas and tied them around their horses' and mules' muzzles, in a futile attempt to provide them some relief from the constant dust. However, those bandannas helped men and mounts but little. The fine dust managed to filter its way through even the most thickly doubled fabric, to settle deep in throats and lungs.

They slapped dust from their clothes, beat their hats

against their legs to knock dust from them, and, when they attempted to drink from their canteens, swallowed as much dust as they did water.

"This dust botherin' you, Nate?" Jeb asked him, one afternoon.

"It ain't the dust so much as it is all this sand," Nate answered. "With this much sand, there's gotta be a beach around here somewhere."

"This ain't Delaware," Jeb answered, laughing. "All you'll find in these parts is more sand. The only Beach around here is Shorty."

With places ideal for a drygulching becoming more frequent, all the Rangers were constantly on alert. Percy and one or two other men rode ahead of the rest every day, searching out possible trouble.

Without even realizing it, Nate had begun to develop the skills and survival instincts crucial to staying alive as a lawman in the vast, lonely, lawless expanses of Texas. Under the brim of his Stetson, his eyes were constantly moving, looking for something out of place, seeking out anything which didn't seem quite right. His hearing also became more attuned to his surroundings, especially at night.

Percy had taught him it wasn't when you heard the sounds of the night creatures, the chirping of the crickets, the rough call of the cicadas, the rustling of a mouse, the hooting of an owl, the howl of the wolf or the cry of the cougar that you had to worry. It was when those creatures went silent you had to be concerned.

Percy had explained you could even follow a man creeping up on you in the dark by listening to the night critters. As a man passed by their hiding places, they would go silent, then start up again once he had moved on. Follow the rising and falling of the night creatures' voices, and you could track, fairly accurately, anyone attempting to sneak up on you in the night.

As the days passed, Nate also noticed subtle changes in his body. He'd grown a couple of inches, making him appear even lankier. What little fat he'd had was now gone, to be replaced by muscle; muscle that hardened with each mile of riding. Except for the pain of the knife slash along his ribs, he no longer ached at the end of the day, and wasn't stiff and sore the next morning.

He could stand his turn at watch without becoming drowsy, was handling the *remuda* with more and more ease, and was even able to snatch a few minutes of sleep while he rode.

Thirst and hunger, while constant companions, no longer tormented him as they once had. He could go for hours without taking a swallow from his canteen, ride all day on only a few bites of jerky and hardtack.

Despite the protection of his wide-brimmed hat, his face was no longer white and pale, but tanned, and becoming tough as leather from constant exposure to the sun and wind, as was the back of his neck and the backs of his hands. The only light skin above his shoulders at all was a clearly defined white ring across the top of his forehead, where the sweatband of his hat rested.

His palms, once soft, easily blistered, were now thick and calloused. Fine wrinkles were developing around his eyes, from constantly squinting in the harsh light of the desert. He sometimes wondered if his mother, father, or brother would even recognize him, had they still been alive.

This third day after Nate and Percy's fight with the Comanches, the Rangers had come across a fairly good-sized spring, issuing from the base of a low mesa, so Captain Quincy called an early halt for the night, two hours before sundown.

The spring formed a small pond, just large enough for washing, which was drained by a small creek that disappeared into the sinks less than a quarter-mile away.

After making sure the horses had drunk their fills, then themselves, and George had obtained sufficient water for cooking and brewing coffee, the men took turns cleaning up; some just their faces, hands, hair, and necks, others stripping out of their shirts to scrub dust, grit, and grime from their upper torsos.

Even Shorty Beach, who usually avoided water as if he had hydrophobia, cleaned up. When Nate's turn came, he shrugged out of his shirt, dunked his head into the water, then began scrubbing his face. When he ran his hands over his cheeks and chin, some of what he thought was dirt refused to wash away. He scrubbed harder, with the same results. When the dirt still remained, he uttered a mild curse.

"What's the matter, Nate?" Hoot asked. He had just finished washing.

"I know cactus needles can stick to a man…" Nate began.

"Yeah, you sure found that out durin' your horse race with Andy," Hoot interrupted, laughing at the memory of Nate and Andy Pratt, who had been killed in the ambush on the Ranger camp, flying from their horses and landing on their rumps in cactus patches. Jim Kelly had taken quite a few cactus spines out of their butts, much to Nate and Andy's chagrin, and the rest of the Rangers' amusement.

"You ain't ever gonna let me live that down, are you,

Hoot?" Nate asked. He'd slid into using "ain't", like the rest of the men, instead of the proper "aren't" he'd been taught in school back in Wilmington. He was sounding more and more like a native Texan every day.

"No, pard, I certainly ain't," Hoot replied. "Now, what are you carryin' on about?"

"This dirt stuck to my face. I can't seem to get rid of it, no matter how hard I try."

Hoot looked closer at Nate's face, then chortled.

"Nate, I don't know how to tell you this, but that ain't exactly dirt you're tryin' to get rid of."

"It ain't? Then what the heck is it?"

"Them's whiskers, pal."

"Whiskers?"

"Yeah. Whiskers," Hoot confirmed. "Appears to me you're startin' to grow yourself a beard."

"Whiskers?" Nate repeated. He ran a hand over his face once again. Sure enough, he was sprouting a beard. The whiskers were fine in texture and light in color, little more than peach fuzz, but they were there, nonetheless.

Whiskers. He hadn't really noticed before, but now that Hoot pointed out he was growing whiskers, he realized hair was starting to show on other parts of his body, under his arms, a bit on his chest, even on some other, more private areas.

Evidently, along with everything else that had happened over the past few weeks, his body had decided it was time to leave boyhood behind, and start becoming a full-grown man. He shook his head. "Whiskers."

"Yeah, whiskers," Hoot said. "You can find yourself a lookin' glass and admire 'em when we get to Fort Stockton," he said. "Meanwhile, I'm plumb starved. Let's help George get set up, so he can start supper."

"All right." Nate pulled his shirt back on, then he and Hoot headed to the chuck wagon. They gathered downed mesquite branches for the fire, then helped George unload his pots, utensils, and dishes.

• • •

After supper, as usual, most of the men, except those on sentry duty, hung around the campfire, working on final cups of coffee, smoking, and swapping stories and tall tales. Joe Duffy usually broke out his harmonica to play a few tunes.

After helping George clean up the dishes, Nate took his sketch pad and pencils from his saddlebags, then found a quiet corner, away from the rest of the men. He leaned back against a rock, then opened the pad and began to draw. He worked, undisturbed, for nearly an hour, until Tom Tomlinson wandered over. Nate glanced up from his work.

"Hey there, Tom. I didn't see you sneakin' up on me," he said. "You look awful tired. You feelin' all right?"

"Sorry, Nate. I didn't realize you were concentratin' so hard you didn't notice me comin' over. I'm all right, I guess. Just kinda missin' Tim a bit more'n usual tonight."

Tom's twin brother, Tim, had been killed by a duplicitous deputy sheriff, who had been working hand-in-hand with the outlaw gang which had ambushed the Rangers—the same gang which had attacked Nate's home and murdered his family. Tim had managed to kill the traitorous deputy before he died.

"I can understand that," Nate said. "Some days I miss Jonathan really fierce, more even than my ma and pa."

"Same here. I hadn't seen my ma or pa in over three years, but me'n Tim rode side by side as Rangers for nearly two years, until he got killed. I sure miss him. Along with bein' my brother, he was my best friend."

Tom sighed, then glanced down at the pad Nate held.

"What'cha up to, Nate?" he asked.

"Just doin' a little drawin'," Nate answered. "I used to do a lot of it back in Delaware, but this is the first chance I've had to try it again, since my family moved to Texas."

"Do you mind if I take a look?" Tom asked.

"No, not at all." Nate turned the pad so Tom could see his drawing.

"Nate, that's real pretty," he said. "Looks like you've got all of us in there, mostly."

Nate had sketched a picture of the company, while they sat around the fire.

"I'm not all that good," Nate said, with a shrug. "Drawin's just somethin' I like to do."

"I dunno, Nate. That picture looks real nice, at least to me," Tom answered. "You mind if the rest of the fellers take a look?"

Before Nate could reply, he shouted. "Hey, Cap'n Dan. Lieutenant Bob, and the rest of you fellers. C'mon over here and take a gander at what our pal Nate's been doin'."

"Tom, I ain't all that good," Nate repeated.

"We'll let the rest of the fellers decide that," Tom answered.

"What's goin' on, Tom?" Captain Quincy asked, when he reached him. The others were right behind, their curiosity piqued.

"Appears like we've got us a gen-you-wine artiste in our midst, Cap'n," Tom answered. "Show him, Nate."

"All right." Reluctantly, Nate handed his pad to the captain.

"You drew this, Nate?" Quincy asked.

93

"Yeah," Nate answered. "It ain't all that much."

"On the contrary, Nate, this is quite good," Quincy said. "Take a look, men." He held up the sketch for everyone to see.

"Hey, that's us," Shorty Beach exclaimed.

"It sure is," Jeb Rollins added. "You really drew that, Nate?"

"Yup."

"I think it's fine," Jeb said. "You got a whole lotta detail in there, the sunset, George's wagon, the brush, the packs and saddles on the ground, even a couple of the horses. And us, of course."

"Right down to the smoke and flames of the fire," Larry Cannon added.

"You been drawin' for long, Nate?" Quincy asked.

"Off and on since I was a kid," Nate answered. "Haven't done much of it since I came to Texas."

"Well, you've got a real talent for it, son. That's for certain," Quincy said.

"Dan, I've got an idea," Lieutenant Berkeley said.

"What is it, Bob?"

"How about we make Nate our official company artist? He can do sketches of us ridin' along, of everyplace we go, some of the people we meet, mebbe even some of the fights we have. Someday, when we're all long dead and gone, it would be a record of what we've accomplished out here. What do you think of that?"

"I think it's a fine idea, except for the part about drawin' our gun battles," Quincy answered. "I don't think Nate'd be able to sketch and fight renegades at the same time. He'd have his hands full just keepin' from gettin' shot, and tryin' to plug the men tryin' to put a bullet in him. There's a big difference between drawin' a picture and drawin' a gun."

"I know that, Dan," Bob retorted. "However, he could draw from memory, after everythin' is over. And mebbe he could do pictures of any of the men who might want one, to send back home to their families and loved ones. What d'ya say, Dan?"

"I think it's a fine idea, but it's more important what Nate thinks," Quincy answered. "How about it, son? Would you be willin' to record the company's history, in pictures?"

"I wouldn't mind, Cap'n," Nate answered. "I still don't think my drawin's all that good, though."

"You let us, and anyone else who sees your work, be the judges of that," Quincy added. "And there'll be one other benefit for you, also. Since you'll be appointed the official company artist, and I guess that also makes you the company historian, I'll be able to reimburse you for the cost of your drawing supplies. Now, is this picture just about complete?"

"Yeah, Cap'n. All I have to do is sign my name to it."

"Good. You do that, then I'll place this drawing in my files for safekeeping. After that, it's high time we all turned in for the night. Dawn'll be here before you know it."

"And not the *Dawn* you're thinkin' about, Dakota—that pretty lady you fell for back in Fort Worth," Jim said, laughing. Dakota shot him a look that could kill.

"All right, that's enough. Time to hit your blankets," Quincy ordered.

• ● •

Just before they fell asleep, Hoot called to Nate.

"Pardner, you still awake?" he whispered.

"I wasn't, but I am now," Nate grumbled. He rolled onto

his side. "What d'ya want, Hoot?"

"I sure wish I could draw like you," Hoot answered. "I can whittle some, but I was never much with a paper and pencil. I was wonderin', when you get the chance, could you draw a bunch of pictures of me?"

"Sure, I'd be glad to," Nate answered. "But why do you need a whole bunch? Wouldn't one or two be enough?"

"One or two ain't nearly enough," Hoot said. "I want to give one to each gal I leave behind. With all the gals I meet, and who naturally fall in love with me, I'm gonna need a whole lotta pictures."

"Hoot, I ain't never seen a gal fall in love with you yet," Nate retorted. "Heck, I ain't seen one even kiss you, let alone fall in love with you."

"It'll happen, Nate," Hoot said. "You can bet your hat on it."

"Hoot, go to sleep," Nate said, yawning. "Mebbe you can get a gal in your dreams, 'cause that's the only way you're ever gonna get one, pal... in your dreams. Now, good night."

He rolled onto his back, pulled his Stetson over his eyes, and ignored Hoot's cursing, spluttering response.

• • •

The next morning, as they were readying to leave, Percy approached Captain Quincy.

"Cap'n," he said. "Thanks to those Comanches who jumped me'n Nate, we never did get the men those antelope we promised 'em. You mind if I take Nate along and see if we can scare up a couple today?"

"No, I don't mind one bit," Quincy answered. "Have you asked Nate if he wants to ride with you again?"

"I did, just a few minutes ago. He's eager to go, and

learn a bit about huntin'. Last time he didn't get much of a chance."

"Except on how to hunt and fight Indians," Quincy said.

"That's for certain. He did get an unexpected lesson in that," Percy agreed. "As long as we have your permission, I'll get him, and we'll head on out."

"Go right ahead, and good luck. There's just one thing."

"What's that, Cap'n?"

"Try to stick with pronghorns this time, Percy. Don't go chousin' any more Comanches or Apaches out of the brush."

"I'll do my best, Cap'n," Percy answered, matching the captain's laugh with one of his own. "Yes sir, I'll do my best." Still laughing, he headed over to where his horse, already saddled, waited, and where Nate was tossing his saddle on Big Red's back.

"You about ready to ride, Nate?" he asked.

"Just about. Only have to get my cinches tightened and Big Red's bridle on," Nate answered. "Captain Quincy said it was all right for me to go with you?"

"He did. In fact, he thought it was a right fine idea."

"That's good." Nate finished tacking up, then swung into his saddle. "I'm ready, Percy."

"Then let's go." They put their horses into a walk, and rode out of camp.

• • •

Nate and Percy rode most of the morning, without any sign of game at all. Just before midday, Percy reined in Wind Runner. In front of them was a wash, which had a trickle of water running down its middle. Mesquite, and even a few far out of place, stunted cottonwoods, grew

97

thickly along its banks.

"Nate, I'm bettin' if we follow this wash, it'll widen out after a bit," he said. "And I'm thinkin' we'll find some pronghorns where it does."

Nate looked up and down the wash.

"Yeah, I can guess why. There's water, and grass. In fact, this'd be a good spot to make camp for the night, if it was a little further along toward sundown."

"Nope, you're right about the water and grass, but wrong about settin' up camp in this wash, or any wash, for that matter," Percy answered. "You don't ever camp in a dry wash, not ever, unless you're desperate, and there's no other place to stop."

"Why's that, Percy?"

"Take a look to the northwest, the direction this here wash comes from. You see those low mountains and ridges up that way, off in the distance, on the horizon?"

"Yeah, I see 'em."

"Good. Now, do you see those clouds buildin' up over those hills?"

"Yeah. Those white, fluffy clouds sure are pretty against the deep blue sky."

"They're pretty right now," Percy said, "but in a few hours, there's a good chance they won't be so pretty. Odds are those clouds will build up into a whopper of a thunderstorm by later this afternoon. They'll dump an awful lot of rain over those hills, rain which will come roarin' outta there, fillin' up this wash, brim to brim. That's the reason we call storms like that gullywashers. They send down flash floods, with little or no warnin'. Sure, the sun might be shinin' here, but in those hills it'll be rainin' like the dickens.

"If you're caught in a wash when one of those floods

bursts through it, you don't have a chance. You'd be drowned before you even knew what hit you. So, tempting as it might be to camp alongside that creek, with the shade from the mesquite and the grass for your horse, and water for the both of you, you don't ever want to do it. *Comprende?*"

"*Comprende*, and then some, Percy."

"Good. Oh, and there's another reason I think we'll find some pronghorns before too long. The grass has been dried up for weeks, except along this wash, but all that mesquite is bound to tempt our quarry. Those are honey mesquites. The leaves and pods are mighty temptin' to most grazin' animals. In fact, the pods are pretty tasty for us humans, too, and we can also eat the leaves if we have too. Keep that in mind."

"All right. Let's go find our supper."

Percy urged Wind Runner down the sandy slope and into the wash, with Nate and Big Red following close behind. They rode for about half a mile, when Percy motioned for Nate to stop.

"Shh, Nate. There they are, right ahead."

Percy pointed to where the wash widened and petered out, merging with the plain. A herd of about twenty pronghorns was nibbling at grass and mesquite.

"We'll leave the horses here, and go in on foot," Percy whispered. He motioned for Nate to dismount. "Quiet as you can. We don't want to scare 'em off."

They swung from their saddles, and tied the horses to a good-sized mesquite. Both mounts fell to munching on its pods and leaves. Nate and Percy pulled their rifles from the saddle boots.

"Pronghorns are real skittish animals, Nate. We've gotta be real careful stalkin' 'em, as the least little thing might spook 'em. We'll use the mesquite and scrub for cover. You stay close behind me, but not so close you can't see a dry stick, step on it and snap it, or send a loose rock clatterin'. That'd stampede those ornery critters for certain. Lever a round into your gun's chamber now, otherwise the sound's liable to scare 'em off."

Nate nodded his understanding. He jacked a shell into his Winchester's chamber, then followed Percy as he made his way silently through the brush.

When they were about a hundred yards from the pronghorn herd, Percy dropped to his belly. Nate did the same, pulling himself along with his elbows until he was alongside the scout.

The pronghorn acting as sentry jerked his head around, sniffing the air suspiciously. Percy put a cautioning hand on Nate's shoulder. Both men remained motionless, until the sentry relaxed a bit, and turned his attention in the opposite direction, apparently convinced nothing was amiss.

"All right, Nate," Percy said. "See those two, with their sides to us? Those are the ones we want. I'll take the one on the left. You need to aim just behind your animal's shoulder. That will put your bullet in its heart or lungs, for a quick, clean kill. There's hardly any breeze, so you don't need to worry about allowin' for the wind workin' on your shot. Just don't forget to aim a bit higher than your target, though. Your bullet will drop some, but not all that much at this distance.

"Aim for just below its spine, and you should make a good hit. We'll have to shoot at the same time, otherwise one of us'll miss when the rest of the herd takes off. You ready?"

Nate nodded. He eased his rifle forward, and placed it

against his shoulder. Alongside him, Percy did the same. He nodded at Nate, then both eased back their triggers, squeezed, and fired. Panicked by the reports, the prong- horns bounded away, racing across the plain, leaving two of their number behind. Percy's target had dropped in its tracks, while Nate's stumbled two steps, fell to its knees, rolled onto its side, thrashed for a moment, then lay still.

"Good shootin', Nate," Percy said. "Let's get the horses, and go pick up our supper."

They retrieved their mounts, then led them up to the kill.

"We'll load them on the horses, and head back to find the outfit," Percy said.

"We're not gonna butcher them here?" Nate asked.

"No. With that storm buildin' up on the rimrock, we don't have time. We need to get back to the others, and have 'em quicken their pace. They need to know there's a flood comin'. If we don't get across this wash before it fills, we could be stuck here for two or three days. I'll show you how to tie your kill on Red."

"How about leavin' 'em here, and pickin' 'em up on our way by?"

"The coyotes and buzzards'll have made short work of the carcasses, long before we get back. Look."

Percy pointed at several black specks, circling in the sky.

"Buzzards? Where'd they come from?" Nate asked.

"They survive on carrion. They can spot a dead animal, or human, from miles away," Percy answered. "Let's get these critters loaded up."

"All right." Red snorted and shied at the sight of the dead pronghorn and the smell of its blood, but Nate was able to calm him enough so the animal could be draped over Red's rump, and tied in place. The other pronghorn was tied over Wind Runner's rump, then Percy and Nate mounted and pointed their horses in the direction from which they'd come.

"That was a good shot," Percy repeated. "You hit your target right in the lungs. You sure don't want to just wound an animal, then have to chase it down, or worse, lose it and have it die slow, after sufferin' a lot."

"Thanks, Percy," Nate mumbled.

"You seem kinda quiet, Nate," Percy said. "A little bit down. Somethin' botherin' you?"

"Mebbe a little. It just made me a bit sad, seein' this pronghorn die from my bullet. I know we have to kill to eat, and survive, but I can't help feelin' a bit sorry for him."

"It's good you feel like that," Percy answered. "That shows you have a respect for all creatures, unlike, say, the buffalo hunters, who kill bison by the hundreds just for their hides, and some of the choice meat, then leave the rest to rot. The Great Spirit provided animals for men to use, and to eat, but not to squander needlessly. You'll be just fine, Nate."

"Thanks, Percy."

"Just one more thing. You might hear it said that Indians have a saying, 'It's a good day to die', or 'That pronghorn, or buffalo, or deer, is showin' himself because he's ready to die, or it's his day to die'. Well, maybe some Indian somewhere at some time said that, but I ain't never met one who did. There's no day that's ever a good day to die.

"These pronghorns we just shot sure didn't want to die, and I certainly don't want to die, except of old age, in my bed. So if anyone ever tries to tell you it's a good day to die you look him straight in the eye and say, "Bull—"

"I get your meaning, Percy," Nate said. He broke into a

smile. "And I shot my first antelope. Mebbe I'll make it out here, after all."

"None of us ever had any doubt about that, kid. Well, perhaps a few."

Percy kicked his horse into a lope.

• ● •

"Riders approachin', Cap'n," Jeb Rollins called. "Appears it's Percy and Nate. Looks like their horses are carryin' somethin' besides them, too. I'll wager we eat good tonight."

Once Percy and Nate drew nearer, the men could make out the pronghorns draped over their horses' rumps. They let out a cheer.

"We eat better'n bacon and beans tonight, boys!" Carl Swan yelled.

"Appears to me like you eat good every night there, Carl," Hank Glynn answered.

"Mebbe I do, but if we ever get lost out here and run outta grub, I'll still be alive long after you skinny hombres have starved," Carl retorted. "That's why I keep this extra meat on my bones."

The Rangers had come to a stop. Percy and Nate rode up to them.

"I see your hunt was successful, Percy," Captain Quincy said.

"It certainly was," Percy replied. "Nate and I each got us a nice, fat pronghorn. There's fresh meat tonight."

"Well, then thanks to the both of you. We'll make camp as soon as possible."

"We can't, at least not until we cover some more distance," Percy answered. "We shot these animals in a good-sized wash, a few miles ahead. There's a storm buildin' over the rimrock to the north. If it gets as large as I suspect it's goin' to, that wash is gonna flood, and stay in flood for a couple of days. If we don't want to get stuck waitin' for the water to recede before we can get movin' again, we need to cross that wash before the flood hits."

"You reckon we have enough time to beat the flood?" Lieutenant Berkeley asked.

"We should have plenty," Percy answered. "It'll take the storm a couple of hours to form, at least, then it'll be another two or three before the water gets this far. As long as we don't dawdle, we'll make it with ease."

"Then we'd better get movin'," Quincy said. He waved the column forward.

"Rangers, Ho! At a lope."

• ● •

The Rangers were safely eight miles beyond the wash by the time the storm broke in the hills, so they never saw the wall of debris-laden water which came roaring down it, carrying away everything in its path. Instead, they had made camp with the anticipation of fresh meat for supper, in place of the ordinary bacon, beans, and biscuits. The pronghorns Percy and Nate had killed were butchered, cut up, and the pieces spitted over a large fire.

"I know we shouldn't have a fire this big, since it'll be spotted by any renegades or Indians within twenty miles of here," Captain Quincy said. "However, we don't get to eat this well very often, and we sure don't want any of this meat to go to waste. We'll just have to keep an extra sharp lookout tonight."

The men settled down to their meal, eating with gusto. Fresh meat, be it venison, fowl such as partridge or quail, even the infrequent wild pig or javelina, was always a welcome treat on the trail. Most of them were a bit more than halfway finished when Ken Demarest, who had the first watch on sentry duty along with Hank Glynn, called out a warning.

"Riders comin' in. Appears to be about ten or so."

Immediately, every man became alert, setting aside their plates, coming to their feet, and placing their hands on the butts of their six-guns. George picked up his rifle from the tailgate of the chuck wagon.

"Just take it easy, boys, until we see who they are," Captain Quincy cautioned. "But be ready for anything."

"They appear to be a company of dang bluebellies," Ken shouted, when the riders came closer, and he got a better look. "Seems like they don't mean trouble."

"Bluebellies? What are those?" Nate asked Hoot.

"Yankee soldiers. That's what most of us call 'em down here," Hoot answered. "There ain't a lot of love lost between most folks in Texas and the United States Army, and that includes us Rangers."

The end of Reconstruction, with its scalawags and carpetbaggers, its onerous laws intended to punish the South for seceding from the Union, its crooked politicians and high taxes, which had forced many people off land which had been in their families for generations, had occurred not all that many months ago. Its memory was still bitter in the minds of many Texans.

While the Army's string of forts across Texas was now meant to provide protection from raiding Indians, most sons and daughters of the Lone Star State would prefer to handle the Indian problem on their own. There was also nearly constant friction between the Army and the Rangers.

"Hoot, just keep those thoughts to yourself," Quincy

ordered. "As for the rest of you, it doesn't matter whether you like the Army or not, I don't want any trouble with these men. Let's just see what they want."

Several of the men grumbled unintelligibly, but none went against his command.

"Hello, the camp," the man leading the column of soldiers called as they drew near. He wore a captain's insignias. "Mind if we come on in?"

"C'mon in, but slow and easy," Captain Quincy replied.

"All right."

The soldiers rode cautiously into the Ranger camp. Except for the captain, all were black men.

"That captain's the only white man. The rest of those soldiers are blacks," Nate said.

"They're buffalo soldiers," Jeb explained. "Most of 'em are freed slaves, along with a few men from the North who weren't ever owned by anyone. The Indians gave 'em the name *buffalo soldiers*. They believe the hair on those men resembles the hair on a buffalo, all crinkly like it is. Buffalo soldiers are some of the toughest, hardest-fightin' men you'll ever come across. I'd be happy to have some of 'em sidin' me in a fight with the Comanch', Apache, or Kiowa any time."

The soldiers reined their horses to a halt. The captain gave a brief salute.

"Captain Terence Anders, at your service. These men and I are with Company A, 9th Cavalry, stationed at Fort Stockton."

Anders spoke in a clipped Massachusetts accent. From his speech and bearing, he apparently was from a wealthy family, and was probably a graduate of West Point.

"Captain David Quincy, Company C, Texas Rangers. This is quite the coincidence, Captain Anders. We're headed for Fort Stockton, then further into the Big Bend."

"A happy circumstance indeed," Anders replied. "We saw your fire, but what really piqued our interest was the smell of meat being roasted. Would it be too presumptuous of me to ask if you have enough to share with a patrol of hungry soldiers? It's been far too long since we had fresh meat."

"Not at all. I understand completely. This is also the first meat, other than bacon or jerky, we've had for quite some time. We have plenty to go around. Get down off your horses, and light and set a spell."

"You are most gracious, Captain Quincy. May I present my second in command, Sergeant Travis Burnham."

The burly man at Anders's right nodded.

"Pleased to meet you, Sergeant," Quincy said. "As soon as your men care for their horses, we'll have their supper ready. Phil Knight, that tall beanpole standin' next to the fire, is our chief hostler. He'll show you where to picket your mounts."

Burnham saluted. "Much obliged, Cap'n." He ordered the other troopers, "Company, dismount!" Following Phil, they led the horses away.

• ● •

The cavalrymen kept mostly to themselves, making some small talk with the Rangers, but mainly eating in silence. Captain Quincy and Captain Anders, after finishing their meals, were smoking cigars Anders had provided, and drinking coffee.

"What're you doin' out this far east, Captain?" Quincy asked. "I didn't realize men from Fort Stockton patrolled this area."

"We ordinarily don't," Anders answered. "As you know,

the Army's main duties here in Texas are to prevent any depredations by the Comanches and Kiowas. However, there have been quite a few raids, by a particularly vicious band of white outlaws, taking place in this region recently. With no state authorities in the area, we took on the task of trying to locate the gang, and apprehend them."

"Do you have any idea who you might be after?"

"As far as names, no. We only have a description of some of the members, and their *modus operandi*. That means their method of operation."

"I know what it means, Captain."

"You do? Excellent. Anyway, to continue, these men have no compunction at all about killing, whether their victims are men, women, or children. They will attack an isolated ranch, murder everyone there, loot it of goods and livestock, then burn it to the ground. They'll disappear for a few days, perhaps even a couple of weeks, then pop up somewhere far distant from their last raid. They have left few witnesses alive to provide any clues as to their identities.

"However, there have been several who did manage to hide from their attackers, or played dead to survive. We know there are ten or twelve, perhaps a few more, in the band. One of them is a half-breed. Another is a big, burly man, quite possibly a Cajun from his appearance.

"The man who is apparently the leader is quite fair, in fact, from some of the descriptions we have, he could possibly be an albino. His hair is so blond as to appear almost white. His skin is also very light; one person even described it as the color of flour. His eyes are an extremely pale blue. He's also quite the fancy dresser. Wears a broad-brimmed white hat, brightly colored shirts, and favors flashy silk neckerchiefs. One person stated he wore twin pearl-handled Colts; however, we haven't been able to confirm that."

Nate was sitting on a log a few feet from the two offices, sketching them while they conversed. He dropped his sketch pad and looked up at them.

"Cap'n Quincy! That's got to be the same bunch that murdered my family, and then ambushed us," he exclaimed. Nate's eyes glittered with hatred, along with excitement at the thought they might finally have a lead as to where to find those cold-blooded killers.

"Just rein in a minute there, Nate," Quincy said. "We can't be certain."

To Anders, he continued, "Nate and his family were attacked by a gang whose leader closely matches the man you just described. His mother, father, and older brother were all killed in the raid. Nate was shot and left for dead. Their ranch was burned down, and all the livestock rustled. The same outfit later ambushed us, killed six of our men, and wounded several others, including Nate. If the men you are searching for are indeed the same ones, not only Nate, but all of us Rangers have a score to settle with them."

"I'm confident they are, from what you just told me," Anders answered. "The methods are exactly the same, and apparently the descriptions are a good match."

"What was their last whereabouts?" Quincy asked.

"They attacked a ranch about forty miles southeast of here," Anders answered. "We managed to pick up their tracks and followed them south toward Del Rio. We trailed them quite a ways, but lost them somewhere in the Devil's River breaks. My opinion would be they make their headquarters somewhere in that vicinity."

"That would make sense," Quincy said. "That's mighty

rough country. It'd be a good place for an outfit that size to hole up. Tell me, though, Captain. Why'd you turn back, rather'n pushin' on after those men?"

Anders shrugged, almost apologetically.

"We had no choice. We'd already pursued them too far, and for too long. We have orders to be back at Fort Stockton so another patrol can go out. In fact, we're already two days overdue. I don't need to tell you my commanding officer will be starting to wonder what has happened to us. Major Zenas Randall Bliss expects his orders to be followed to the letter. He is also not a man to sit around and do nothing, if he feels any of the men under his command might have run into trouble. I have two or three more days, tops, before he sends out a search party. And if that happens, it will be a blot on my record."

"I hardly think so, once the major finds out you were attempting to bring in a bunch of *muy malo hombres*," Quincy protested. "Out here, a man sticks with a job until it's done."

"Then I'm afraid you don't know the United States Army very well, Captain. Orders are not to be taken lightly, and disobeying them requires very extenuating circumstances. The Army's mission in Texas, and most of the West, is to solve the Indian problem, not handle state and local law enforcement. I had no choice but to give up the pursuit."

"Cap'n Quincy, with all due respect to you and Captain Anders, those have got to be the men we want," Nate broke in. "Just sittin' here talkin' won't do any good. We have to go after 'em. We have to."

"Nate, just like Captain Anders has his orders, we have ours," Quincy replied. "We're supposed to get to the Big Bend, as quickly as possible. And odds are, even if those are the same men, they're no longer near where Captain

Anders broke off his pursuit. They've either fled for other, safer, parts, probably Mexico, or are off somewhere on another raid."

"But, Cap'n—"

"Just hold on a minute, son, and let me finish. Unlike Captain Anders, I can change plans if circumstances warrant. That's why we're called Rangers, 'cause we range all over the state, stoppin' trouble wherever we find it. I reckon the Big Bend can wait a few more days, while we go after those renegades. It'll mean some backtrackin', since we've already gone quite a ways past the Devil's River, but we're gonna hunt down those men. They've raided their last ranch, and committed their last murders.

"Besides, the Devil's River country *is* kinda on the eastern edge of the Big Bend, at least close enough so I can stretch the truth a bit, and convince Headquarters we were in the territory when we started chasin' that gang.

Captain Quincy turned to look at Anders once more. "We'll ride out at first light. Captain Anders, thank you for the information. You've finally given us a solid lead as to where to locate that outfit. You and your men are welcome to stay the night with us, of course."

Despite his disgust with Anders for letting a gang of thieves, rustlers, and murderers slip from his grasp, Quincy knew it was imperative for the Rangers to maintain cordial relations with the Army, as much as possible. Otherwise, there was still the possibility Washington could reimpose martial law, or perhaps even an extension of the hated Reconstruction laws, on Texas again. That would once again place the state under the jurisdiction of Federal troops.

He choked back what he would really like to say to the Army captain, resisted the temptation to tell Anders exactly where he could shove those orders and how to do it, and fixed a smile on his face.

"That's most gracious of you, Captain," Anders replied. "We'll be happy to accept your offer. And the best of luck in finding those outlaws."

"Oh, we *will* find 'em, Captain. You can bet your hat on that," Quincy answered. "Nate, gather up the rest of the men. I need to tell them our plans have changed."

"Right away, Cap'n."

It only took Nate a few moments to inform the other Rangers Captain Quincy was calling a meeting. The look on his face and the tension in his voice made it obvious something important was happening. The men were soon grouped in front of their captain.

"Men," Quincy said. "Captain Anders and his troopers have been pursuing the men who attacked Nate and his family, and ambushed us, killing six of our comrades.

"However, they lost their trail and were forced to turn back, due to Army regulations. Captain Anders did obtain good information as to where those men probably make their hide-out, down along the Devil's River. We'll be starting after them first thing tomorrow morning."

A mutter of satisfaction swept through the men, before Quincy could continue.

"We'll be riding fast and hard. That means, George, we'll be traveling without you. You'll remain here until we return. I want one man to stay with you. Do I have any volunteers?"

As he expected, he got nothing but silence in return.

"That's exactly what I figured. Lee, Larry, since you're new to the outfit, and weren't with us when we were ambushed, neither of you has quite the stake in finding those renegades as the rest of us. I'm going to have you draw cards. Low card stays behind. Carl, I know you weren't either, but you did tangle with the outfit at the Lopez ranch, so I figure you've got a score to settle with 'em too."

Cannon and Shelton nodded their understanding. George took a deck of cards from the wagon. He handed them to Quincy, who shuffled them, cut them, and held them out to the two new men. Cannon drew first.

"Six of clubs."

Shelton chose his card.

"Ten of diamonds. Looks like I ride."

"That's settled," Quincy said. "Now, everyone get a good night's rest. We have a tough few days ahead of us."

"All right, Dav," Lieutenant Bob said. "You heard the cap'n, boys. Turn in."

Most of the men were soon stretched out under their blankets. Captain Quincy had just slid under his when Sergeant Burnham approached.

"Cap'n, I hope I'm not disturbin' you," he said, in a voice surprisingly soft for such a big man. His accent placed him as from somewhere in the deep South, most likely Georgia or Mississippi. "I just need to speak with you for a moment."

"Not at all, Sergeant," Quincy replied. "What's on your mind?"

"I just had to let you know it wasn't the men's decision to stop searchin' for those outlaws. We wanted to keep after 'em, but Cap'n Anders ordered us to turn back. It's not that he isn't a brave man, because he sure is. I've fought several battles with him. He's a real hard fighter, and a good leader. Me and the rest of the men under his command would follow him into Hades and back. But, he's a West Pointer, and goes strictly by the book. So, when he realized if we kept after those men we'd be way overdue gettin' back to Fort Stockton, he made us turn around. Just wanted you to know that."

"I appreciate that, Sergeant," Quincy answered. "And please be aware, I would never have questioned you buffalo soldiers' dedication or courage. I know of your reputation, and what kind of fightin' men you are, first hand."

"Thank you, Cap'n. I'll bid you good evenin', now. And good luck in roundin' up that gang."

"Much obliged, Sergeant. Good night."

• • •

On the other side of the camp, Nate was trying to fall asleep, knowing he needed to get as much rest as he could before they started out at sunup. But, his mind kept racing. His body was tense with anticipation. At last, would this be the final confrontation with the murderers who had taken everything from him, except his life?

Nate tossed and turned for an hour, before finally falling into a fitful sleep, a sleep broken for the rest of the night by a dream. A dream which kept repeating itself. A dream in which he and the pasty-skinned, pale-eyed son of Satan who was responsible for the murder of his family came face to face for one final time.

The dream always ended the same way. Nate and the killer drew their guns and fired.

Gunsmoke blotted out Nate's vision, and a sharp pain shot through his chest. He woke up drenched with sweat, his heart pounding, and his guts in a knot.

5

Three days later, two hours before dusk, Captain Quincy called a halt for the night. They were just leaving the level plain they'd been crossing, and approaching an area of low hills. To the right of the trail was a shallow stream.

"Men, I know this ain't a very likely lookin' campsite, but we're not gonna ride any further, with dark comin' on," he said. "I've fought outlaws in these parts before. That's the Devil's River over there. It might not look like much from here, but let me tell you, it's a pretty good sized stream a bit further south.

"These hills are only gonna get more rugged from here on in. The vegetation's gonna get thicker, too, the deeper we ride into the river breaks. There's even places where cottonwoods and cedars grow good and big. There's a lot of canyons cuttin' the land. That means there's plenty of places we could ride straight into a drygulchin', if we got caught nappin'.

"At night, if those renegades are in there, they could pick all of us off, real easy. We'll spend the night here, then go on in first thing in the mornin'."

"Do you really think those men are in there somewhere,

Cap'n?" Carl asked.

"Quien sabe?" Quincy shrugged. "Who knows? We have no way of knowin' for certain. For an outlaw gang, this is ideal territory. Plenty of canyons and hills to hide in, and lots of places to set up an ambush. But if they are in there, I've got a good idea where we'll come up with 'em.

"About six miles south of here is Brushy Draw. That'll be to the left of the trail. Directly opposite that is Sycamore Canyon, and right next to that is Hudspeth Springs. If I were an outlaw, that's where I'd hole up. It'd be real hard for anyone to find a man in there, and even harder to get one out. Lots of cover. Even quite a few of the trees are big enough to hide a man bent on a drygulchin'.

"Any of you boys who were in the War, you know what we're up against. Think of how many of your friends were picked off by Yankee snipers. This is the same situation. That's why we'll wait until mornin'. At least, with daylight, we'll have some chance of spottin' those men before they spot us. If we went in after dark, we'd just be ridin' blind, and askin' for bullets in our backs."

"There is one other option, Cap'n," Percy spoke up.

"If there is, I'd like to hear it, Percy."

"We'll camp here, as you said. Once it's full dark, I'll scout ahead, and see if I can find any sign of those men. I'll go on foot, so there's no chance anyone would spot my horse. At least, that way, we'll have some idea what we're up against, or if we've just been sent on a wild goose chase."

"Percy's got a good idea there, Dan," Bob said.

"I've gotta agree with the lieutenant," Jeb added.

Quincy stroked his chin. "I dunno. It's awful risky. I'd hate losin' you, Percy. Far as I'm concerned, you're the best scout in the Rangers."

"Thanks, Cap'n. Which means I won't get caught. And if those men are in there, I can give you at least a pretty good idea of where they're situated. Besides, that's what the Rangers pay me for, to be a scout. I don't need to remind you an Indian can slip around without bein' heard or seen far more easily than a white man."

"All right, you've convinced me. Soon as it's full dark, you go ahead. There's no moon tonight, so that will help. The rest of you, care for your horses, then make sure your weapons are in good working order. It'll be a cold camp tonight. Supper'll have to be jerky and hardtack. No coffee. We can't chance a fire. It'd be too easy to spot. All right, dismount."

• • •

Not one of the men turned in early that night. They all were alert, even the men not on sentry duty watching for any signs of the outlaws. Captain Quincy had ordered no smoking, lest a cigarette's glow or chance puff of smoke drifting to a renegade's nose give them away. That meant no one could calm his nerves with the comfort of tobacco.

Everyone was anxiously awaiting Percy's return. Nate was the most tense of all. He spent an hour grooming Big Red, currying him over and over.

"Nate," Hoot finally said, "You brush that horse any more you're gonna take all the hide right offa him. What's the matter with you, anyway? You're more nervous than a long-tailed cat in a room full of rockin' chairs. I figured you'd gotten over your fright by now."

"I dunno," Nate said. "I'm not sure if I'm afraid that Percy will find signs those men are here, or if he won't. I'd hate to think we came this close, only to find we're on the wrong trail."

"Well, you can't do nothin' until he gets back," Hoot said. "No point stewin' about it. You want to draw some of those pictures for me while we're waitin'?"

"It's kinda hard to sketch in the dark," Nate answered, chuckling. "Don't worry about me, Hoot. I'll be okay."

"I sure hope so, pard. Meantime, it's ten o'clock. That means it's my turn on watch, along with Hank. Reckon I'd best find him so we can get out there to relieve Joe and Dakota."

Hoot picked up his rifle to start up the ridge where Captain Quincy had stationed the sentries. He'd only gone a few yards when Dakota met him.

"What're you doin' down here already?" Hoot asked him.

"Percy's comin' in. Reckon we'll know now what we're up against," Dakota said.

Nate had seen Dakota walk into camp. He dropped Red's currycomb and hurried up to him.

"Did I hear you right, Dakota? Percy's back?"

"He'll be here in a minute or two. Better let him talk to the cap'n first, though, son."

"I guess you're right," Nate reluctantly agreed. He, along with the others, watched until Percy emerged from the gloom. The scout headed directly for where Captain Quincy stood, waiting.

"Well, Percy?"

Percy uncapped his canteen and took a long swallow of water before replying.

"They're in there, all right. I found the tracks of at least a dozen horses, cuttin' off this main trail. My guess is they belong to the men we're after. Whoever's leadin' the outfit is a right smart hombre, too. Half the hoof prints head into Brushy Draw, the rest into Sycamore Canyon. We'll have to split our forces to go after all of 'em."

"Funny they didn't try'n hide their trail," Dan said.

"Not all that funny," Percy answered. "They probably figure anyone who sees those prints'll just reckon they belong to cowboys searchin' for cattle. Or, if anyone does think they belong to rustlers or smugglers, they sure as heck ain't gonna go in after 'em. That'd be plumb loco. Heck, it's gonna be plumb loco *us* goin' in there."

"You think they have a guard out?" Jim asked.

"Wouldn't you?" Percy answered. "I got close enough to spot at least one. That's how I'm positive these are the same men who ambushed us. The hombre on watch is a big man, kinda dark-skinned. I'd bet dollars to doughnuts he's the Cajun Captain Anders talked about."

"Good work, Percy," Quincy praised. "Boys, we'll start out an hour before sunup. Bob, you'll take Jim, Percy, Dan, Hoot, Joe, Hank, and Ken. Your job will be to clean out the snakes in Sycamore Canyon. I'll take Jeb, Tom, Phil, Dakota, Carl, Lee, Shorty, and Nate. We'll go after the ones in Brushy Draw. We'll hit those men soon as it's daylight. From what I know of those canyons, this most likely won't be an all out assault. We might get a couple of those men right off, but after that it'll be a guerilla operation. We'll have to roust those hombres out from wherever they're hidin', behind trees or rocks, dug into the dirt, wherever we find 'em, one man at a time. I don't need to tell any of you to be careful. Make sure you don't shoot one of your pardners by mistake. Any questions?"

There were none.

"Good. Now, try and get some sleep. And may God ride with us and protect us."

• • •

It seemed to Nate he had barely fallen asleep before Hoot was shaking his shoulder. He'd spent most of the night staring at the sky, questioning what would happen when he and the Rangers finally confronted the men who had murdered his family, ambushed the Rangers, killing six of them, and attacked the Lopez ranch, killing two more innocent cowboys.

And who knew how many other robberies, killings, burnings, and lootings these men had committed? All Nate's fears came roaring back, with a vengeance. Would he be able to face the pale-eyed outlaw leader he'd vowed to kill, or would he turn tail and run? Or would he freeze, and let the man finally put a killing bullet into him?

Try as he might, the answers wouldn't come. He finally dozed off, still wondering.

"C'mon, pardner, rise and shine," Hoot said. "Time to get after that bunch."

Nate threw back his blankets and sat up. "All right, Hoot. Sure wish you were sidin' me, rather'n ridin' with Lieutenant Bob."

"Hey, you can't always count on me bein' there to pull you out of every scrape you get into," Hoot said. "Don't worry, Nate. You'll be just fine. I wouldn't say that if I didn't believe it."

"Thanks, Hoot. Reckon I'd better saddle up."

There would be no breakfast this morning. The men contented themselves with water from their canteens. They saddled and bridled their horses in silence, mounted, and started off, the only sounds the soft clopping of the horses' hooves, the creaking of leather, and the occasional jingle of a bit chain.

The air had cooled considerably overnight, and a thick mist had formed over the Devil's River. It hugged the ground like a thick blanket of cotton. A slight breeze pushed it over the trail, sending it swirling through the brush, up the canyons and into the draws, swaddling the brush and trees.

By the time the Rangers reached the junction with Brushy Draw and Sycamore Canyon, the mist had thickened even more, limiting visibility considerably.

Silently, Captain Quincy waved Bob and his men into Sycamore Canyon, then led his own into Brushy Draw.

"Keep a sharp lookout," he whispered. "You can be certain there's at least one man watchin' for anyone snoopin' around. Don't stay bunched up. Spread out a bit."

Despite the chill in the air, sweat was beading on Nate's forehead. It dampened the armpits of his shirt, and trickled down his back and chest.

When a shot rang out, he jerked in his saddle. Ahead of him, Shorty Beach toppled from his horse. More bullets ripped through the brush. Behind them, more gunfire crackled from Sycamore Canyon.

"Get down!" Captain Quincy shouted. He grabbed his rifle and rolled from his saddle. The rest of the men followed his lead, pulling the rifles from their boots, jumping off their horses, sending them to safety with slaps on the rump, then diving for cover.

As soon as he hit the ground, Captain Quincy got off a shot at the drygulcher who had gotten Shorty. His quick shot hit the outlaw in the middle of his chest, penetrating his heart and killing him instantly.

Bullets were ripping through the brush, seeking out their targets. Men screamed in pain whenever one found its mark. Nate dove to his belly and crawled forward, as lead split the air all around him. He spotted one man hiding behind the trunk of a cottonwood, just his left side exposed. He took careful aim and fired.

The man staggered from behind the tree when Nate's bullet took him in the side. Nate levered and fired again, this bullet striking the outlaw just above his belt buckle. The man screamed, dropped his gun, grabbed his middle, then pitched to his face.

A bullet from behind him took off a branch, just above Nate's head. He rolled onto his back, to see the big Cajun Captain Anders and Percy had described taking deliberate aim at his chest. He tried to bring his rifle to bear on the man, knowing he could never aim and fire before the outlaw put a slug into him.

Just as the Cajun pulled his trigger, another shot rang out, plowing into the outlaw's back and slamming him forward. Blood spurted from the man's chest where the bullet exited. The impact lifted him off his feet, then he spun a half-circle and crumpled onto his side.

Lee Shelton, his smoking six-gun in his hand, grinned at Nate, then disappeared into the scrub.

Between the fog, the thick brush, and the confusion of the fight, Nate soon lost track of time, place, and his companions. He kept pushing forward, dodging bullets, searching for more of the outlaws.

The battle raged for what seemed, to him, like hours, but which was, in truth, less than thirty minutes. He came to an opening in the brush, in the middle of which lay a body, face-down and motionless.

Nate crawled up to the dead man and rolled him over. Lee Shelton had died with three bullets in his chest. Nate got sick to his stomach. Another bullet smacked into the dirt alongside him. Nate scrambled back into the brush.

The gunfire was diminishing now, only an occasional shot echoing through the draw. *Who was winning?* Nate wondered. *Were most of the outlaws dead, or was it most of his partners who had fallen with bullets in them, and was he soon to join them?*

His thoughts were interrupted by a shout from just ahead.

"Rangers. I've got your captain. The only way you'll see him alive again is if you ride on outta here, then let me and my men head for Mexico."

"That's him!" Nate exclaimed to himself. "I'd know that voice anywhere. It's the son of Satan who leads this bunch." He came to his feet and ran straight for the voice. He burst out of the brush to find the pale-eyed gang leader with one arm around Captain Quincy's neck, and his hand holding a gun to the captain's head.

"Nate!" Quincy shouted. "Get outta here, kid."

Nate shook his head. "Can't do it, Cap'n." He dropped his rifle and placed his hand on the butt of his Smith and Wesson.

"You'd better find the rest of your buddies, and tell 'em if they're not outta here in five minutes your captain's a dead man," the outlaw leader said.

"Not gonna happen," Nate answered. "Don't you know who I am, mister?"

The pale-eyed outlaw squinted as he looked more closely at Nate.

"*You!* The kid we thought we killed back outside San Saba. The kid I thought I gunned down in the Ranger camp. Well, your luck just ran out, sonny boy. I'm gonna make *sure* of you this time."

Furious at seeing Nate still alive, thinking of nothing but finally shooting him dead, the outlaw shoved Captain Quincy aside, and brought his gun around.

Before he could thumb back his hammer and pull the

trigger, Nate lifted his gun from its holster and shot him twice in the chest. The man staggered backward, but didn't fall. He was bringing his gun level when Nate shot him in the belly. The man grunted, buckled slightly, but still managed to get off a shot, which just missed Nate's left ear.

Nate tossed aside everything which Jeb had taught him about aiming for the biggest target. He aimed lower, and put a bullet into the pale-eyed Satan's groin, dropping him to his knees.

With only two bullets left, Nate aimed carefully, and shot the outlaw right between his eyes. The man twisted and fell onto his back. Nate stalked up to him, kicked the gun from his hand, and watched the light fade from those pale eyes.

He walked over to where Quincy lay, struggling to rise. The gunfire had now completely stopped.

"You all right, Cap'n?" he asked.

"Yeah. I'm okay," Quincy answered. "Just twisted my ankle when that hombre shoved me to the dirt. Help me up, will you?

"All right." Nate helped Quincy to his feet. The captain leaned against him for support.

"How about you, Nate? Are you okay?"

"I believe I am, Cap'n, yes."

"What about that pale-eyed devil?"

"He's dead. I made sure of it this time. It wasn't easy, though. My first three bullets didn't seem to bother him, hardly at all."

"I saw what happened, son. Let's see why. Gimme a hand gettin' over to him."

"All right."

Quincy, with Nate's help, hobbled over to the dead

outlaw.

"There doesn't seem to be any blood on his shirt, Nate. Open it up and let's see why."

"Sure." Nate opened the outlaw's shirt. Underneath it was a thick garment, which appeared to have two outer layers of silk, with several alternating layers of silk and a cotton-like material in between. Nate's bullets were stuck in the garment. There were also several patches where the outlaw had evidently been shot previously.

Quincy let out a low whistle.

"Well, I'll be. Never seen anythin' like that before," Quincy said.

"Explains why my bullets never hurt him," Nate said. "But I need to check one more thing."

He rolled the outlaw onto his back and pulled down his shirt collar. At the right side of the base of his neck was a fading bullet scar.

"I knew it. I did get him, back at the Lopez place," Nate said. "If it hadn't been for that lightnin'..."

"There's no time to worry about that now, Nate," Quincy said. "We've got to find out what's happened to the rest of the boys. If they haven't taken care of what's left of this bunch, they'll be comin' after us."

"I don't think we have to worry about that, Cap'n. Look."

Jeb and Dakota emerged from the brush, guns still at the ready.

"Over here, men!" Quincy called.

"Cap'n. You all right?" Jeb called back.

"We're both fine," Quincy answered. "The leader of this outfit's lyin' dead, over there. Nate plugged him."

"Nate? Good work, boy," Dakota said.

"Let that go for now," Quincy answered. "How about the

others? And the rest of us?"

"Far as we can tell, they're all done for, at least on our side of the trail," Jeb answered. "If there are any we missed, they've turned tail and run. Haven't seen Lieutenant Bob yet, so can't say as to what happened in Sycamore Canyon. We did lose one man. Shorty Beach was killed by that bushwhack shot. And one's missin'. Lee."

"Lee's dead," Nate answered. "He's lyin' in a clearing over that way." His lower lip trembled, his voice cracked, and his eyes filled with tears. "He saved my life. The big Cajun was about to plug me, but Lee got him instead. And now, he's dead."

"There's nothin' to be done about it," Quincy said. "Riskin' your life just goes with bein' a Ranger. Lee knew that when he signed on. He wouldn't want us frettin' about him. Same goes for Shorty. He died doin' what he loved best…upholdin' the law. Now, we'd better find out what happened to Bob and his men."

• • •

Lieutenant Berkeley and his men had also routed the outlaws who were hiding in Sycamore Canyon. Captain Quincy and the surviving Rangers from his group found them halfway into the canyon. Two of the men were stretched out on the ground. Jim was working on one.

"Hoot!" Nate shouted, realizing his friend was the man Jim was treating. Hoot's face was coated with blood. "What happened to you?"

"I made a dumb mistake," Hoot said. "Stepped in front of a bullet. Never, and I mean *never*, do that, Nate."

"I reckon that's good advice," Nate answered. "Too bad you didn't give it to me sooner. I did get plugged when this gang attacked my family's ranch, and again durin' the ambush on our camp, remember? You gonna be all right?"

"Hoot'll be just fine, Nate," Jim said. "The bullet just grazed his thick skull. Wish I could say the same for ol' Hank, but I can't. He took two slugs through his guts. He didn't have a chance, but at least he took the man who killed him with him... the half-breed who was the *segundo* of the outfit. Hank nailed him plumb center, before he went down. Drilled him right through the stomach."

"Then it appears this gang is finished," Quincy said. "We'll patch up our hurts, and bury our dead soon as we can. As far as the outlaws, we'll just leave 'em for the buzzards and coyotes. Even that's more'n they deserve."

"You reckon we'll find some identification on any of 'em, Cap'n?" Jeb asked.

"Don't matter to me if we do or we don't," Quincy replied. "Far as I'm concerned, it's better if no one ever finds out their names. They don't deserve to be made into legends, or some kind of folk heroes. Best they're just forgotten, and disappear into the sands of time."

• ● •

The Rangers spent the night at Hudspeth Springs. Shorty Beach, Hank Glynn, and Lee Shelton were buried just before sunset, with rocks placed over their graves to discourage any scavengers, and crude wooden crosses set at the heads of their final resting places. Captain Quincy said a few words, commending their souls to the Lord.

"Poor Shorty," George said, as his friend's body was lowered into the grave. "He never got a chance to break in those new drawers proper." The other men laughed, their sorrow broken, if only briefly, at George's humorous tribute.

After supper, Quincy assembled the surviving men,

and called Nate to the front. He held a cloth-wrapped bundle.

"Nate," he said. "I have something here which belongs to you." He handed Nate the bundle. Nate opened it, to find a pair of silver spurs, with his brother's initials engraved on them.

"Jonathan's spurs!" Nate exclaimed. "How?"

"We took those spurs off your brother's boots," Quincy explained. "That was before we realized you were alive. We intended to send any valuables from your family back to any relatives we could find.

"They were packed away in George's wagon. In the confusion of finding you, I completely forgot about them. I was going to mail them to you back in Delaware. Then, when you turned up with Jeb, I decided to hold on to them, and give them to you once I was certain you'd make it as a Texas Ranger. Today was that day.

"Nathaniel Stewart, you earned those spurs this day, and you earned the right to be a full-fledged Texas Ranger, age and regulations be hanged. Congratulations, son. You are one heckuva Ranger to fight with."

"Cap'n, I—I don't know what to say," Nate stammered. "Thank you. Well, and does this mean I don't have to help George gather firewood anymore?"

"Don't push your luck, son," Quincy answered, laughing. "I do need to know your plans, now that the men who murdered your family are dead. Will you be heading back East, or remaining here, in Texas?"

"Cap'n, as long as the Rangers will have me, I'll stick with 'em," Nate said. "They're the only family I've got, now."

"I knew you would, Nate," Hoot hollered. "That means I'll still have the chance to get you smokin' yet."

"Men, it's been a long day, and we've lost three of our comrades," Quincy said. "Let's give a yell for Nate, then call it a night."

The Rangers' shouts shattered the stillness of the night air.

• ● •

Before he turned in, Nate took out his sketch pad, and found a spot behind some scattered boulders, out of sight of the rest of the men. He sketched a picture of the pale-eyed son of Satan who had led the outlaw gang which took his family.

The drawing showed him lying dead, with Nate's bullet holes in him. Nate stared at the picture for quite some time, then pulled his bundle of lucifers from his shirt pocket, broke one off, lit it, and touched it to one corner of the paper.

He held the drawing as the flames consumed it, and watched the ashes float into the air. Never again would that devil torture him.

Nate would never forget what the outlaw and his followers had done to his family, what they had taken away from him.

But no longer would that pale-eyed raider be a demon, tormenting his every waking moment. Nate had made certain of that.

Page 70: The College of the Immaculate Conception was the forerunner to present-day Loyola University.

About the Author

Jim Griffin became enamored of the Texas Rangers from watching the TV series, Tales of the Texas Rangers, as a youngster. He grew to be an avid student and collector of Rangers' artifacts, memorabilia and other items. His collection is now housed in the Texas Ranger Hall of Fame and Museum in Waco.

His quest for authenticity in his writing has taken him to the famous Old West towns of, Pecos, Deadwood, Cheyenne, Tombstone and numerous others. While Jim's books are fiction, he strives to keep them as accurate as possible within the realm of fiction.

A graduate of Southern Connecticut State University, Jim now divides his time between Branford, Connecticut and Keene, New Hampshire when he isn't travelling around the west.

A devoted and enthusiastic horseman, Jim bought his first horse when he was a junior in college. He has owned several American Paint horses. He is a member of the Connecticut Horse Council Volunteer Horse Patrol, an organization which assists the state park Rangers with patrolling parks and forests.

Jim's books are traditional Westerns in the best sense of the term, portraying strong heroes with good character and moral values. Highly reminiscent of the pulp westerns of yesteryear, the heroes and villains are clearly separated.

Jim was initially inspired to write at the urging of friend and author James Reasoner. After the successful publication of his first book, Trouble Rides the Texas Pacific, published in 2005, Jim was encouraged to continue his writing.

Lone Star Ranger Series

A Ranger to Ride With

A Ranger to Reckon With

A Ranger to Fight With

A Ranger's Christmas

A Ranger to Stand With

A Ranger Gone Bad

A Ranger Redeemed

A Ranger Grown

A Ranger Returns

A Ranger for Life

A Ranger Never Quits

A Ranger at Peace

Made in the USA
Columbia, SC
02 December 2024

47364763R00074